MW00874952

TOXIC

CRAVINGS #3

BY
RACHAEL
ORMAN

Toxic

Copyright 2015 by Rachael Orman

Toxic is a work of fiction. Names, characters, places, and incidents are either the product of the author's imagination or are used fictitiously. Any resemblance to actual persons, living or dead, events, or locales is entirely coincidental

Acknowledgements

To my husband & babies – Thank you for always supporting me in everything I do! Couldn't ask for better behaved children or more loving spouse!

Jacqui - As always the first to get my book, the first to give me support, the first to start messaging on me for more… Love ya lady!

Editing Juggernaut – Love you for putting up with my stupid errors and pointing out my funny mistakes.

Phycel Designs – Thank you for creating the perfect cover for the final book in the series… It's exactly what I wanted!

Chapter One

~Alix~

"Precious," John called from the dining room.

I quickly wiped my hands on a kitchen towel before dropping it back to the counter and going to him.

"The guests should be arriving soon," he informed me even though I already knew.

We were expecting about a dozen of his friends from "Scene", the BDSM club we frequented. I had only briefly met most of the people so I was nervous. It was our housewarming party. After living together for six months in John's previous apartment, we'd made the big decision to buy a house together. To be honest, I hadn't wanted a party, but John had insisted.

"Come here, Precious," John instructed me with a half-smile tugging the corner of his lips up.

I nervously wiped the sweat from my hands on the skirt of my flowy knee-length dress. Master always made me nervous. It was a good thing though. I never knew what he had in store for me, and I loved it — almost as much as I loved him.

Once I got within three feet of him, I sank to my knees with my head bowed.

"Yes, sir?" I asked quietly.

"Precious, stand up. Lift your dress for me," he said. He patiently waited for me to rise and do as I'd been told.

I lifted my hem up so he could view the garter belt and thigh-highs I had on under the dress. No panties.

"Beautiful," he breathed before pulling me into his arms. Placing a soft kiss against my cheek, he was careful to not mess up the lipstick he insisted I wear for the party. His thumb skimmed over my cheek while his hand cupped my neck, his brilliant blue eyes meeting mine for a moment. Then without another word, he released me and moved to pull a stool I hadn't noticed from the corner.

On top of the bar-height wooden chair was a flesh-colored dildo. It was stuck to the seat with a suction cup and glistened, already lubed, in the light from the chandelier over the table.

"Please, have a seat." John smiled and held out his hand for mine.

I ran my eyes over him even as I slipped my hand into his. His short, light brown hair was perfectly in place as always. He wore a suit jacket and pants with a white button down shirt, which gaped slightly at the top where he'd left a few buttons undone. Just laying my eyes on him heated my insides. Then when he spoke and I heard his faint British accent, I was done for. I'd never recover if something bad happened between us. Not simply because he was my master, but because he had become my everything in the time we'd been together.

I had to release his hand to lift my dress again from where it had fallen on the one side as I stepped in front of the stool. I'd never sat on a dildo before, but I'd do anything he had planned as he always made it worthwhile in the end.

"Lean forward," he said as he pressed a firm hand on my upper back. Slowly he helped me take the lubed dildo all the way in. Stepping back, he draped my skirt around me so that no one would be able to see that I was impaled while sitting at the table. He walked around the table, keeping an eye on me as he went. "Yes, I think that will work perfectly. You look beautiful sitting there like that."

"Thank you, sir," I said, folding my hands in my lap and lowering my head.

The doorbell rang, drawing our attention.

"Looks like the evening is ready to begin." John gave me a final smile before heading off to greet the first of our visitors.

In no time at all, we had a house full of guests. Some had stopped by the dining room to greet me, but John had told them I wasn't permitted to greet guests at the door so no one thought much of my inability to move from the dining room or even stand.

Once everyone had arrived, John ushered them all into the dining room to their seats. If I'd thought I was uncomfortable before, it was ten times worse with a room full of people I hardly knew while stretched and filled with the dildo.

John made sure to touch me in one way or another every chance he had, though, which relaxed me. A brush against my back, arm or thigh was all it took to remind me that Master would always take care of me.

When everyone had found a seat and had a drink, he returned to the kitchen to get food. I tracked him with my eyes as he went, dropping off plates to each guest. It was something I would normally handle, but he'd taken that out of my hands and I felt guilty for not being able to serve him and our guests. Some of them looked curiously from John to me a few times.

All of their curiosity was satisfied, however, when John finally took his seat, clicked a remote in his pocket — and the dildo came to life.

The vibrations weren't something that could've been easily hidden in the quiet chatter in the room. My surprised gasp was probably all it would've taken for this group to know something was going on anyway.

Turning my head, I met John's glittering gaze as he forked more food into his mouth in an attempt to hide his smirk. I couldn't even feign a glare as the vibrations were doing what they were designed to do. I hadn't been turned on when I'd first started this game with John, but now I wanted to rotate my hips and make the dildo move more than it was.

Maybe I should've been embarrassed it was in front of a room full of people; then again, I'd done worse before at the club. I just hadn't expected our party to take this turn of events. Not to mention I was still fully dressed and no one other than John and I knew exactly what was going on.

And *that* was what turned me on the most. I looked around quickly at the other guests, but no one was paying me particular attention. They all had smirks or half-smiles letting me know they were aware of what was going on, though.

John's hand settling on my knee startled me enough to make me meet his eyes again. He held up a fork-ful of food for me, which I took and chewed quickly so I could swallow it. Breathing was more important than eating right then.

I struggled to keep my breathing even as I felt my orgasm growing close. Just when I thought I wasn't going to be able to hold back, the vibrations stopped and I almost collapsed forward in relief, but John was there with another mouthful of food. I wasn't hungry, but I ate it anyway.

The rest of dinner progressed in spurts of the vibrator being turned on or off at random intervals, and by the time everyone was done eating I was ready to fuck on the table in front of everyone, I was so turned on. Then John went and offered everyone dessert or coffee.

I nearly groaned in frustration, but one look from John and I bit my lip to control myself.

Finally, everyone was done with their refreshments and catching up with each other. Just as quickly as they'd arrived, our guests left with a few nods in my direction.

With John out of the room seeing the last of them out, I was tempted to lean forward on the chair and ride the dildo until I got off. I didn't. I knew John wouldn't be happy if I got myself off after all his teasing.

4

I was still forbidden from getting myself off, even though I had managed to keep my addiction under control since we'd moved in together.

John strode back into the room. His jacket was missing and he was in the process of removing a cufflink when he stopped on the other side of the table from me. He dropped the first one to the table before undoing the second and setting it next to its mate. Then he smiled as he tapped the button in his pocket, bringing the vibrator to life once more.

"Mmm. Do you know how hard I've been all evening knowing that you are sitting on a cock?" he asked as he moved closer to me. Calmly he rolled up one sleeve to his elbow, then the other. One hand glided up my back until his fingers sank into my hair and he tugged my head to one side. His warm, moist lips brushed my ear as ho whispered, "All I wanted to do was slide my dick into you and make you scream out for me in front of our table filled with guests dressed in their fancy clothes. Make you soak the front of my pants with your come while all of them watched and got hot and hard themselves."

I shivered at the image he painted. I wish he would have done it. My pussy clamped down around the toy inside me at the thought.

John's fingers glided over the column of my neck before following the strap of my dress down to the zipper at the back. He slowly pulled it down, filling the room with the soft metallic clicks of it coming undone. With a soft kiss on my shoulder, he released my hair to pull the hem of my dress over my head, leaving me in only my garter belt and stockings.

"I do love your creamy skin," John whispered as his hands moved over my exposed back and around to cup my breasts. "So damn perfect."

"Thank you, sir," I breathed. A gasp escaped when he pinched my nipples tightly between his finger and thumb.

I wanted to beg for more, but didn't. He'd take care of me all on his own.

"Lean forward," he instructed as he used his grip on my tender flesh to help. I rested my palms on the table and spread my thighs wider on the chair so I didn't topple over.

Staring at the table, I felt exposed and alone when he let go of me. However, the snick of plastic let me know he had a container of lube in hand; that was my best guess since I'd heard the sound many times before.

A slippery finger moved against the tight rosette between my cheeks. Without any other warning, John pressed two fingers into my ass and picked up a fast rhythm.

The new angle had pushed the toy deeper inside me, forcing it to rub my g-spot, then the added sensation of him stretching my ass and I was nearly undone.

"Oh, sir!" I moaned, balling my hands in the thick, expensive table-cloth. I fought back my orgasm with everything I had. I didn't want it to end, nor had I been given permission, but I could only do so much. "I'm going to come!"

"No you aren't," he stated as if he were truly in control of my body. Then his fingers were gone and I gasped in a few deep breaths, using the reprieve to bat back my release.

It worked until he was back to teasing my rear entrance. Only it wasn't his finger, but his cock nudging the tight hole. Slowly, he pushed the head of his cock into me and paused.

A scream tore from my throat at the invasion. He hadn't stretched me enough to be ready for him, but after a moment I wanted all of him. I *needed* more of him.

"Sir, more, please," I begged between breaths.

John needed no more encouragement and slammed his hips against mine, seating himself fully in my ass.

"Christ, Precious. You are so tight," John groaned against my neck as he wrapped both arms around my torso. After thrusting deep a few times, he dropped one hand to the table for more leverage as he continued to fill me.

With both my pussy and ass being ravaged, I could barely hold myself together. John's breath against my neck and back along with his soft groans and moans telling me how much he was enjoying it only ratcheted up my own level of pleasure that much more.

"All night I thought about filling you. Fucking you into the table. Pulling on your hair. Sucking your clit into my mouth while you lay naked on the table in front of everyone," John said as his hand on my stomach moved lower to caress the ball of nerves he spoke of.

"Please... Please... Master..." I tried to voice my needs, but it was becoming harder and harder to form words of any kind.

"Come," John barked the single word.

I shattered.

Every muscle, every tendon, every part of my body tensed as I felt pleasure rip through me.

Locking my elbows was the only way I was able to keep from falling forward as my body slowly relaxed and came back together.

John was still pounding into me and groaning louder than before. Suddenly, he pulled out from me. Yanking me off the dildo, he forced me to my knees as he ripped off the condom. A few rough yanks on his shaft and he splashed come onto my breasts.

He liked seeing his release on my skin. Another way of marking me as his.

I leaned forward to lick the last of his release off the tip of his cock. Then I looked down to watch his thick, white strands of semen slide down to get caught on my pearl necklace. The sight pleased me more than it probably should have. Seeing John's collar mixed with the evidence of the pleasure I'd been able to give him almost made me want to beg for more, but I knew I'd be sore after what the evening had been filled with.

"My beautiful Precious. Come, let's shower. We can deal with the dishes later," John said, holding out a hand to help me to my feet.

"Yes, sir," I said, smiling at him.

He pulled me firmly against his still fully-clothed frame and pressed a firm kiss to my lips.

"Have I told you how much I love you?" he asked, resting his forehead against mine.

"Yes, but I wouldn't mind hearing it again," I said with a wink.

"I love you more than my own life. I need you more than I need air. One day soon I will make you mine forever. Maybe then I won't feel the need to make sure everyone knows you are mine every chance I get," he said, cupping the back of my neck.

"I hope you never stop wanting that, sir. I need your dominance as much as I need your love." I closed the distance between us to kiss him softly once more before sliding my fingers into his free hand and pulling him out of the room. "I'd like to wash you now, sir, if you'd come with me."

"I thought we did that already," John said as he followed me.

I could only laugh in response and hope that things stayed exactly the way they were forever. That would be asking too much, though, things never stayed good for long.

Chapter Two

~John~

Another day, another dollar, yes? No. Never seems to be that way for me. My clients always seem to find a way to surprise me. April, the secretary I hired when Jennifer went back to working for the hotel Alix worked at quit, hadn't learned that there was a reason why I liked to allow for more than an hour with each client I met, especially out of the office. I needed that time in case things ran over or to make sure my clients were comfortable after their new experience. And every now and then, people liked to throw in something unexpected, which tended to take longer than expected. With what I'd just been told, I knew, I'd be late to my next appointment.

Jill and Lincoln were the couple I was currently in a session with. They'd wanted to "try something new," like most of the couples I worked with. However, instead of exploring a shoe fetish Lincoln had told me about during our last phone call, he'd decided to ask one of his guy friends to come with him to fulfill one of Jill's requests at the last minute.

I had already prepped Jill in the other room about what to expect when I brought her husband in, but things were definitely going to be going in a different direction with the new addition.

"Does Jill know Mr…" I trailed off not having gotten the other man's name.

"Scott," he supplied.

"Does Jill know Scott? Is she aware this is what you had in mind?" I asked, trying not to let my irritation show. I didn't like surprises. It wasn't how I operated. However, since the couple had been talking about doing a threesome

9

for as long as I'd been seeing them, I didn't want to say it wasn't going to happen if they'd found a willing third.

"Yes, she knows him. Yes, she will be more than willing to fuck him. No, she doesn't know I had asked him to join us, but I doubt it'll be a problem," Lincoln said, running a hand over his thinning brown hair.

"Just so we're clear, how far is he allowed to go?" I tucked my hands in my trouser pockets.

"What do you mean? Whatever he wants to do. Whatever she wants him to do," Lincoln answered like it was me who didn't know what I was talking about.

"So, it's okay if he touches her? Fucks her? Sticks his dick in her ass? In her mouth? Does he need to use a condom? What if he wants to fuck her ass while you fill her pussy? Or her mouth while you screw her? Maybe he'll want to do her while she sucks you off?" I listed off a few of the scenarios that popped instantly to mind. There were many more I could've said, but those were more kinky than things would likely go. It didn't sit right with me for a husband to say that it was okay for another man to do "whatever" he wanted to his wife without a talk about more specifics before-hand. That's how fights started and feelings got hurt.

Before he could answer my questions, I continued, "What about afterwards? Is this a one-off? Does it happen again if one person wants it to? Or does everyone need to be in agreement? Do you have to be present if the two of them want to meet up again?"

"Uh…" Lincoln didn't seem to have really put that much thought into exactly how emotional threesomes could be.

"I think for now we can say it's a one-off. If once it's over anyone wants to talk about it happening again, that'll be the time to sit down and talk about how to go about things from there," Scott answered for his friend. "As for what I'm going to do to her, I think it would be a good idea to know so I don't get a fist to the face for doing something wrong."

I nodded in agreement. I liked him.

"Okay... Okay... How about she can blow you while I bang her and you can only be in her vagina if she asks and with a condom? If she wants to do something more she can ask at the time." Lincoln blew out a long breath as he wiped his palms on his pants.

"Very well. Let me go inform her of the change and prepare her," I stated, then walked to the hotel room next door. After knocking once, I opened the door with the key she'd given me earlier.

Jill was standing by the foot of the bed in her slinky, sheer pink negligee. She gave me a hesitant smile when she saw I was alone.

"Is something wrong?" she asked, wringing her hands together.

"Depends on how you look at it," I sat on the bed and patted the comforter for her to sit next to me. Once she did, I looked into her eyes. "Scott is here and he'd like to join Lincoln in pleasuring you."

"He is?" She jumped off the bed, pacing for a moment before looking back at me.

"Yes. You can say no. It is up to you whether he comes in at all and what he does. Your husband has agreed to let him have sex with you and for you to go down on him if you'd like as well. However, you get the ultimate say in everything, of course." I kept my eyes on hers to make sure she knew I was serious and not at all checking out her scantily-clad body.

"Yes. Yes. I am so interested. I don't know how he got Scott to agree but I am totally on board to any and everything with that man," Jill answered excitedly as she fluffed her hair, then adjusted her outfit unnecessarily.

"Okay. I know you are excited to finally have the chance to explore this fantasy, but I do want to point out

11

that it is best to take things slowly and only do what you are fully comfortable with. Remember your husband will also be in the room and watching you. You don't want to do anything that will hurt your marriage or that will upset your husband," I said, trying to make sure she knew that although a threesome could be great fun, it could also ruin a marriage if everyone wasn't conscious and aware of everyone involved. It was my least favorite fantasy to help couples with because things so often got complicated, but I would help my clients get what they wanted and after that it was up to them where things went from there.

I waited until I was out of the room before letting a sigh go. Something about the whole situation wasn't sitting right with me, but since everyone was on board, there wasn't much else I could do about it. I knocked once, then opened the door to where the men were waiting, and to my surprise they were holding each other locked in what appeared to be a very passionate kiss.

Hearing the door open, they jumped apart. Lincoln's face turned a shade of red while he tried to discreetly wipe a hand over his swollen lips. Scott simply tucked his hands in his pockets, not looking sorry or embarrassed.

"Well, now *this* brings a whole new light to the situation," I said, letting the door close softly behind me.

"We will be telling her," Lincoln jumped in before I could say anything else. "I want to show her how good it could be with Scott around for both of us."

I nodded, glancing between the two men. I wanted to ask questions, but knew that with Jill waiting any delay would only make things awkward.

"We will be discussing this in a one-on-one session, Lincoln. However, you wanted this and everyone else has agreed, so let's go into the room where Jill is waiting." I opened the door and gestured for them to precede me out. Stepping close to Lincoln, I wrapped an arm around his shoulders and spoke softly, "This is a play-by-ear type situation. Pay attention to your wife and see what she is okay with, then go from there. I will be there to help everyone until you all get comfortable."

"All right. I'm ready," Lincoln answered with a nod.

"More than ready over here," Scott added with a smirk.

It was easy to see both men were already aroused.

I nodded before knocking once on Jill's door, and then opened it. All three of us walked into the room.

"Fuck…" Scott breathed at the sight that greeted us.

Jill was completely nude, sitting on the foot of the bed with her legs spread wide. One hand was slowly trailing up and down her abdomen while the other was straight behind her, supporting her on the mattress.

"See something you like?" Jill asked huskily. Slowly her tongue trailed over her plump lips.

"God, yes," Lincoln answered.

As if just noticing her husband was in the room, she flicked her eyes toward him and gave him a half-smile before looking back to Scott.

"How about you, Scott?" She directed the question this time to the man she was asking.

"Oh yeah. My cock is so hard just looking at you."

I wanted to add that he was at least half hard before we entered, but that would be counterproductive so I kept it to myself.

"Show me," Jill demanded as her hand smoothed lower until it pushed through the trimmed, damp curls between her thighs.

Both men groaned as she touched herself. Scott trembled as he attempted to undo his jeans, but finally managed to get the button and zipper undone. His swollen, leaking flesh popped free of his boxers only for him to start stroking himself while he watched her.

"Can I lick him, Linc?" Jill gave her husband a pouty look as she dropped to her knees.

13

"I... If that's what you want," Lincoln stuttered over his reply.

Jill gave him a wide, feral smile before crawling over to Scott. She dragged her tongue from base to tip then moaned as if it was the best-tasting ice cream she'd ever had.

Scott pulled his shirt over his head and threw it aside, which seemed to prompt Lincoln to undress as well.

Not paying attention to anyone, Jill feasted on her treat, licking, sucking, and moaning around Scott. She arched her back, pushing her ass into the air.

I leaned against the wall and watched as their fantasy unfolded. Seemed I wasn't so necessary after all. All they'd really needed was a place and an opportunity while knowing all parties were interested. It didn't happen often, but it was interesting when it did. Once again, like most of my clients, better communication would've solved the issues in the relationship.

Lincoln dropped to his knees behind his wife and pushed his face into her freely-offered ass and pussy. From where I was standing, I couldn't tell which of her holes he was teasing, but by her increased noises she was clearly enjoying the attention he was giving her.

"Fuck yes," Scott said, letting his head drop back as he closed his eyes. Both his hands were gripping Jill's hair as his hips moved in time with her taking him deep in her mouth. Suddenly, he yanked her off him and wrapped a hand around the base of his cock. His erection wilted slightly from how tightly he was gripping it. "Too close. I don't want to come yet."

"Want to watch me suck Linc off?" Jill asked, looking up at him and sitting up straighter.

"No," Linc said, standing. He moved to lie on his back on the bed. "Come ride me and he can whack it while he watches, or touch you... whatever he wants."

A look passed between Linc and Scott, but Jill missed it as she climbed onto the bed and straddled Linc's hips.

"Yeah. Then you can come all over both of us while we fuck," Jill said, biting down on her bottom lip as she looked between her husband and his friend. It was clear she wasn't sure how that suggestion was going to go over, but it was too late to take it back.

"Mmm. Sounds hot," Linc said, nodding in agreement.

Jill reached between their bodies and lined up Linc's cock, then sank down on him in little rocking movements until she'd taken all of him. Leaning forward, she kissed him deeply while rotating her hips.

Scott looked over his shoulder at me as I watched the couple on the bed.

"Sexy, right?" he asked.

"Sure," I said with a small shrug. It really didn't do anything for me, but then again I had a different taste in the bedroom and a woman who brought me to my knees with only a smile or glance in my direction. Seeing clients go at it only made me want to tie up and fuck *my* Alix. Nothing about seeing another man lay his hands on her turned me on, but to each his own. "Why don't you jump in there?"

"Good idea," Scott said, smirking, before walking over to the bed where Linc and Jill were really going at it.

When the bed shifted under his weight, they stopped and both looked toward the new addition. Jill sat up to get a better look at him. Both greeted him with a smile then started moving against each other again, but much slower as they waited to see what he was going to do.

Scott knelt between Linc's legs, ghosting his hands over the other man's skin until he came to where Jill's knees rested. Moving up her thighs, he gripped her ass cheeks and gently pulled them apart. Not happy with her position, he pressed a hand to her lower back, forcing her to lean over Linc again. Then he lowered his head and pressed his face to her puckered entrance and teased it with his tongue.

Moving lower, he used his hand to wrap around Linc's balls while teasing where Linc was filling Jill with his mouth. Both Linc and Jill jumped at the added sensation, but neither stopped moving.

"Yes, Scott. Keep doing that," Linc gasped.

I couldn't see what it was exactly he was doing, but if I had to guess, he was either playing with Linc's perineum or his ass since his hand was no longer visible.

Scott moved back to rim Jill again while continuing to torment Linc.

Faster and faster the couple bucked against each other while Scott dropped a hand to start rubbing his own cock.

"Oh... I'm... I'm gonna come," Linc hoarsely whispered. "Come here, Scott."

Scott moved to kneel next to the couple, but kept his hand between Linc's thighs.

Once he moved I could clearly see he was shoving two fingers in and out of Linc.

"Touch him, Linc," Jill moaned while also wrapping a hand around Scott's length.

Scott massaged one of Jill's breasts while each of them replaced Scott's hand, jerking him off while continuing to rut against each other.

"Yes, like that. Just like that," Jill groaned as Scott pinched one of her nipples while Linc did the same to the other one.

Apparently that was the last any of them could force their brains to put together words as they all fell into moans and cries of pleasure. The trio raced toward their orgasms together until Scott was the first to yell out right before his thick, white come shot out to coat Linc's chest, which seemed to cause a chain reaction. Linc shoved off the bed, nearly unseating Jill as he too shouted out. She rode him until he stopped gasping.

"Mmm, that was fun." Jill smiled at the two men, who were lying on their backs sucking in air as fast as they could.

"Not… acceptable," Linc said between breaths.

"You… didn't… get… off," Scott said, on the same wavelength.

I smiled. At least they were considerate.

After a long moment, Linc rolled until Jill was on her back and he pulled out from her.

"Eat that delicious pussy," Linc directed Scott while moving up on the bed to lie next to Jill.

Scott didn't waste a second before diving between her spread thighs.

I knew he'd be tasting not only Jill, but Linc as well since they hadn't used a condom. From the way he was eating her, he didn't mind. Or maybe he liked it even more because of that fact. They *had* been making out when I'd walked in on them earlier.

It didn't take long for Jill to be writhing on the bed with Scott's tongue lashings when Linc's hand joined in teasing her clit while sucking and nipping at her breasts.

"Yes… Yes… Yeeessss," Jill sighed, dragging out the final word as her body tensed on the bed and her nails dug into each of the men wherever they landed.

I waited a few moments until they were all three cuddled up on the bed whispering to each other in contentment. I would call them later in the day after they had had a chance to recuperate and get themselves together. No need to ruin the afterglow of a good fuck.

Session successfully completed.

As I walked through the lobby of the hotel, I ducked into Alix's office. Unfortunately she wasn't there, so I left her a sticky note on the screen of her computer to call me before heading back to my office next door.

If I'd known what she was dealing with I would've stuck around. Too bad I didn't find out until later.

<u>Chapter Three</u>

~Alix~

The day had started out much like any other day as an event planner for a high-class hotel. More rich kids' parents throwing them parties in our ballroom. More companies putting together meetings in the boardrooms we had. I was booked solid for the entire week, either with appointments with clients to go through what they wanted or to be on hand for an event.

My first client of the day had called and cancelled right before they were scheduled to come in, but I brushed it off. However, when my second and third client did the same thing I became frustrated.

Sitting around for three hours doing nothing when I should've been working sucked. If they'd given me more notice I could've scheduled in other clients during that time, but each had waited until right before their time to cancel.

At least I had more time to prepare for the three meetings that were scheduled that day in various rooms.

When businessmen and women started to filter in for them, though, most gave me odd looks or straight-up glares. I didn't know what I'd done to get the looks, as I didn't even know half of them, but apparently it was something.

I quickly went to the restroom to check my appearance, but nothing was out of place. My skirt suit was still professional — no cleavage or too much thigh showing. It didn't make sense.

After the start time, I ducked into each room and made sure they had everything they needed before heading for the front desk. Thankfully, Jennifer was working.

Ever since she'd introduced me to the world of BDSM we'd become close, even if she didn't enjoy the lifestyle.

"Something strange is going on," I told her.

"Why?" she asked between patrons checking in.

I quickly brought her up to speed on the events of the morning and she frowned.

"That *is* weird. Maybe someone will tell you if you ask?" she said, shrugging as if it was the best idea she had.

I couldn't think of anything else either, but I certainly wasn't going to walk up to someone and ask why they were giving me weird looks. Sighing, I said goodbye and headed back to my office, but I glimpsed a blonde-haired goddess sitting in the lobby. Seeing Mariah, John's ex, stopped me dead in my tracks.

She was flipping through a magazine. As if feeling my eyes on her, she looked up and met my gaze. A broad smile slid across her face as she gave me a girly finger-wave, then turned her attention back to the gossip rag she was reading.

Her appearance left my stomach in knots. I hadn't seen her in months and had thought she'd leave me and John alone since we were living together, but apparently not.

I stared at her for a few moments longer before deciding avoidance was the best course of action for the time being. Maybe it was all a coincidence that she was in the lobby. Yes, she knew I worked there and that John often brought his clients there for their 'sessions,' but perhaps she was meeting someone and it had nothing to do with me or John.

I wouldn't hold my breath, but I would hope.

Returning to my office, I saw I had missed a call. Another client cancelling. At this rate, I'd be getting fired. That thought brought tears to my eyes unexpectedly. I rushed off to the bathroom for a bit of privacy.

It had to be a fluke. Just a bad day. That's all.

Sitting in the stall, I tried to call John, but it went straight to voicemail like it normally did when he was with clients. I hung up without leaving a message. After I had a chance to calm down, I'd try him again or just talk to him when we were at home.

By the time I actually made it home, I was exhausted both physically and emotionally. The day hadn't gotten much better. At least a few of my clients had shown up for their appointments. I even had a few new leads for future events. However, the fact that more than half my day was wasted on waiting for people only to have them cancel had drained me. The last event, a bar mitzvah, had been the kicker. A bunch of little boys trying to pick up on me when their family members weren't watching or trying to sneak booze into the party when they were clearly underage. Not to mention a set of demanding parents that constantly had me running to keep everything up to their standards.

I kicked off my shoes and dropped my purse on the side table by the door. Normally I took them to the bedroom, but I simply didn't care after my day.

At least I found John in the kitchen stirring something deliciously aromatic on the stove when I managed to hobble in.

"Well, hello, Precious," John said, putting down the spoon and wrapping me in a tight hug.

Breathing in his scent and feeling his strength wrapped around me was all the comfort I needed to have the day fade away. I hugged him back while nuzzling into his chest.

"Have a long day?" he asked, rubbing up and down my back with a hand while the other held tight around my waist.

"Mmm hmm," I mumbled against him.

"Go on, kick up your feet. Dinner will be ready soon and then I'll give you a nice foot rub while you soak in the bath."

He always knew exactly what I needed. I sighed happily, but still refused to let go of him. After a long moment, I finally released him so the food didn't burn. I turned to walk out of the kitchen, but his hand on my arm stopped me.

"Hey," he said, hooking a finger under my chin and forcing me to meet his eyes. "Where's my kiss?"

I gave him a soft kiss before pulling back again.

"Everything okay?" His brow creased with concern.

"It is now that I'm home. Just a really long day," I said before striding from the room, not wanting to talk more about it until after dinner. In the bedroom, I changed into my favorite jeans and a tank top before returning to the kitchen.

John had a glass of wine waiting for me. I picked it up and took a long draw from it before sighing.

"Want to talk about it?" John asked, looking over his shoulder while cooking.

"No, John. I don't want to talk about it," I snapped. I was tired and on edge from all the stress I'd been dealing with all day. However, when he flipped the stove off and moved the pan to a cool burner, I knew I'd made a mistake.

He turned slowly to face me. Without a word, he took the glass of wine from my hand and put it on the counter before threading his fingers with mine. He led me to the bedroom and dropped my hand before opening the armoire that held all our toys. Withdrawing a few items, he surprised me by walking into the closet. When he returned he held a pair of my old jeans that I never wore in one hand and a slew of other items in his other hand. He dropped everything on the bed before looking at me again.

"I understand that you had a bad day and for that reason I'm not going to punish you, but I will not allow you to wallow in it the rest of the night. Strip," he said, tucking his hands into his pockets.

Instantly, I pulled my tank top over my head.

"No, just your pants," he said, stopping me.

I tugged the shirt back on before undoing the button and zipper. Why he had me changing jeans I didn't understand, but I figured the reason would be revealed soon enough so I stepped out of them and stood in only my panties, awaiting further instructions.

"Spread your legs," he instructed, taking a step closer to me.

I did as I was told.

John knelt in front of me and I jumped when he slipped something around the big toe on my right foot.

"Breathe, Precious." His warm breath slithered along my panties, making me shiver in anticipation. His fingers slipped into my panties, pulling them aside so he could tease my clit briefly.

"Oh!" I shouted when I felt something bite into my tender flesh. Only then did I look down to see what he'd done, but all I saw was a thin rope running up my leg. Best I could figure was that whatever he'd clamped onto my clit was attached to one end while the other was wrapped around my big toe.

"Now the new jeans," John said, holding them out for me.

I hadn't noticed him standing again or moving to retrieve them from the bed, but I had been momentarily distracted by the pain. It had dulled to something I could easily handle since the initial surprise had worn off.

I stepped into the new pants and fastened them.

John stepped close to me and snapped a handcuff around one wrist.

"Put your hands in your pockets." He waited until I complied, feeling there were no actual "pockets" where there normally would have been – they'd been removed, before undoing the zipper and threading another pair of handcuffs into the opening. He clasped them together to make them longer before securing my other wrist in the opposite side. As he closed my pants again, I realized that my hands were locked into my pockets with very little room to move.

"Now comes the fun part," he said, smiling at me in a way that had every nerve in my body standing on end.

I loved when he took control of me. The look on his face said clearly that I was all his to do with as he pleased.

"These will take away your sight," John said, holding up a pair of sunglasses I'd never seen before. They had padding on the inside of the lenses and when he slid them onto my face they effectively blocked everything out.

He brushed a finger tenderly over my cheek. His fingers wrapped around the side of my neck as he leaned close enough that I could feel his body heat radiating against me.

"You doing okay, Precious?" His lips brushed against my ear as he spoke.

I swallowed hard and nodded once.

"Now I'm going to place something over your lips. You will still be able to breathe through your nose." He rubbed his cheek against mine briefly, telling me without words to trust him to take care of me.

I trusted him with my life so it wasn't even a question in my mind.

Something sticky was placed over my lips and I guessed it was a piece of tape from its texture.

"Last thing."

I heard him move around for a second before I felt something squishy being inserted into my ears. He'd effectively taken away every one of my senses, leaving me completely at his mercy.

He wrapped a jacket around my shoulders before buttoning it closed before putting the hood up over my head. He wrapped my arm around me walked, then led the way out of the room.

Every step I took pulled on my clit from the cord attached to my foot. A gasp tried to escape but without being able to open my mouth I swallowed it back down.

My feet were sore from running around in my heels all day so I was thankful when he helped me into shoes to find they were a comfortable pair of tennis shoes.

Then he walked me out of the house.

I lost track of how long we walked as I was so focused on each step and the tug on my clit that came with it.

Not being able to see, hear, touch, or sense my surroundings was almost frustrating, but knowing that John wouldn't let any harm come to me made it easy for me to relax and my brain finally left behind the stress of work and all the thoughts that had been racing through it.

By the time we returned to the house, I felt like a completely different woman than the one who had left it.

The first thing to come off was the glasses. Seeing John's face made a serene smile come over my own. Then the earplugs came out.

"Better?" he asked, brushing his thumb over my cheek.

I nodded and watched as he unbuttoned the coat before he draped it over the back of the couch.

"Stay here," he murmured before walking out of the room only to return with a washcloth. He used it to delicately take off the tape over my lips. Dropping the washcloth, he tenderly touched my mouth with a finger before folding the barely sticky material and letting it drift to the floor.

John knelt in front of me and placed a kiss on my abdomen while unzipping my pants to undo the handcuffs. With a few more movements my wrists were freed and the pile on the floor grew with the heavy metal. He pulled my pants down to mid-thigh and unclipped my clit, causing me to scream, but his mouth closed over the pulsing flesh as his hand held my panties out of the way.

It didn't take long for the pain to recede and pleasure to take it's place. However, he pulled back with a popping noise and adjusted my underwear so it was comfortable once more before fiddling with the string on my toe.

Once I was completely unwrapped, he pulled my pants up then swept me up to carry me to the couch. Sitting down, he wrapped me in his arms, securing me in his lap.

I buried my nose in my favorite nook between his neck and shoulder and breathed him in deep. After a few moments passed with him holding me in silence, the words poured out of me. I told him all about all the customers I was losing and the possibility of me losing my job.

"Hey…" He hooked a finger under my chin and forced me to meet his eyes. "No matter what happens, we will figure it out. It could be just a bad day. It doesn't matter. Everything works itself out in time. And if by some chance you do lose your job it's not the end of the world. Really. I make plenty of money. It won't be a hardship for me to take care of everything while you look for a new job or even if you decided that you'd rather stay at home, that would be fine too. Money is not an issue. You being happy is the only thing in the world that matters to me. If you are going to be coming home in such a state of panic, maybe it'd be better if you simply quit."

I didn't want that. I loved my job. I was a people-pleaser and loved to see the pure joy that came over a customer's face when I helped fulfil their wishes and dreams. However, I could see his point; I didn't want to be worried about losing my job every day either, but I did want to help pay for my share of the bills.

I sighed and lowered my head back to his chest.

"I know. Can we just eat and forget about the horrible day I had?" I asked. While I had completely forgotten about the day while on our walk, the worry and fear had now started to creep back, but not nearly with the same intensity as before.

"Absolutely. Anything you need, Precious," John said, planting a kiss on my cheek before leading me to the kitchen by the hand so I could watch him finish the dinner he'd been making for us.

Chapter Four

~John~

I hated seeing Alix panic and it was still bothering me days later as I sat in my office waiting for my next appointment to show up. Things had not gotten any better at her job. No one had given a reason or explanation as to why they were all jumping ship so fast; I was beginning to think I knew what was going on, but kept my thoughts to myself until I had more proof.

Alix wouldn't want to be a stay-at-home anything. I knew that, but part of me wished she would do just that. To know that she was waiting on me every day when I got home turned me on like crazy. While we lived the D/s life all the time, it'd be nothing like knowing I could take over that much more of her life. Was it controlling and over-the-top? Probably, but I couldn't help it when it came to Alix. She was everything to me even before she was mine.

One day I would have to tell her everything about myself, but I wanted to put that off as long as I could because I doubted it would go over well. I didn't want to hurt our still-developing relationship. Not when we were still recovering from my psycho ex.

April knocked on my cracked office door before sticking her head in.

"Sir, your next appointment is here," she said in her sugary-sweet voice. The girl looked like she was no more than eighteen, but since I employed her, I knew she was twenty-four.

"Thank you, April." I nodded once and pushed out of my chair. Straightening my jacket, I walked to the door and greeted my next client.

Sadly, it was another woman who had been sexually abused. I saw quite a few women who were trying to get over their past so that they would be able to have a normal sexual relationship, whether they had someone already or were simply thinking about the future. It was the hardest part of my job.

I actually enjoyed helping couples seek out and live their deepest, darkest desires. It fed my dominant side in a way nothing else did. Knowing that I was in control of the situation. That I was the one who'd orchestrated the whole thing. It was heady and gave me a high that was glorious.

Helping emotionally scarred people heal was a challenge I loved as well, though. Everyone was different. Their situations and their feelings about it could never be anticipated. It kept me on my toes and forced me to focus on something outside of my life, my needs, my desires. And it together it all kept me grounded and whole.

The relationship I had with Alix was only the cherry on top. I had started to get burned out before she came along and sparked a new light into my life.

After an hour of trying to help my crying patient, I was happy to have a few minutes break to breathe. It was emotionally draining on me no matter how many people I helped, no matter how many times brutal and cruel situations were rehashed.

April poked her head through the door.

"John, your next patient called and will be a few minutes late," she informed me.

"Thanks," I said. Since I had more time than anticipated, I picked up my phone and dialed Alix to check in on her.

"Hello?" she answered, sounding out of breath.

"Hi, Precious." I smiled and relaxed just hearing her voice.

"Oh, John," she cried.

I heard rustling on the other end of the phone and sat up straighter in my chair. Something was wrong.

"I just met with one of my new contacts and they want me to throw them a swinger party. I've never..." She trailed off and I could hear her gasping, as if she was crying but trying to hide it.

I wasn't sure how to respond. Those were certainly not the type of parties the hotel put together.

"This morning my first new client asked me if they could bring in a Saint Andrew's cross for their party. What is going on?" she wept.

"I have no idea. It's all so strange," I answered, tapping my fingers on my desktop, trying to hold back my anger on her behalf.

"I don't understand why I'm losing respectable clients and having new people come in thinking we throw such parties. Not that there's anything wrong with them, but management will not be happy to hear that word is spreading that these are the types of parties the hotel does."

I sighed. It wasn't that the parties were bad exactly, but a high-class hotel getting a rep for dirty parties would lose all their high-paying clients who didn't want to be associated with such activities.

"We will figure it out. I have a patient who will be arriving soon, but then I have my lunch break and I'll come see you, okay? Just breathe, Precious," I tried to reassure her.

"Okay. Okay," she breathed, then took a much deeper and slower breath. "I'm just really freaking out right now."

"I know, Precious. Just hold it together. I'll be there as soon as I can. I love you."

"I love you too." Then she ended the call.

I glanced at the clock and hoped I had a few more minutes for another call.

***

Turned out my client ended up not being able to make it at all, which was fine by me because I'd needed longer than I'd thought I would for my call and it allowed me to get to Alix sooner.

As soon as I walked into her office, she jumped at me and latched her arms around my neck as she cried into my chest.

Running my hand up and down her back, I spoke soft, calming words to her until she got her tears under control. Finally, I pulled back and nudged her chin up with a finger so she'd look at me.

"It'll be okay. Just remember that I'm here for you no matter what," I said, running a hand through her hair. An idea sprang into my head and I released her to shut her office door before facing her. I moved so I was facing the window out of her office and her back was to it as she followed me. "Lift up your shirt."

She hesitated only a moment before pulling up her silk shirt and revealing her smooth stomach to me. I could see worry in her eyes as I reached around her for the pen container on her desk. Grabbing a Sharpie, I dropped to my knees in front of her before uncapping it.

Carefully I wrote the words "Property of John O'Roarke" over the creamy expanse of her abdomen in large black letters. I recapped the marker and placed a kiss on her skin, then stood. After dropping the pen back on her desk, I cupped her face in both my hands and locked gazes with her.

"Anytime you start to stress out about this nonsense, remember what is written here," I said, splaying a hand over my words. "You are mine. No one else matters. Just me and you, Precious."

"Yes, sir," she breathed as she looked down at the words, then placed a hand over mine. "That helps."

"Good. Now how about we go get some lunch?" I pulled her shirt back down hiding the black marks on her skin.

She took a few deep breaths with her eyes closed before opening them and revealing the more confident woman I had come to know.

"Sounds perfect." She smiled.

Once she'd retrieved her purse, Alix looped her arm through mine and I escorted her out of the hotel, all the unnecessary stress was left behind, at least for a while.

That afternoon when I returned to work I couldn't help but keep going through the conversation I'd had on the phone that morning before seeing Alix. I'd called Mariah and told her that her antics weren't appreciated and weren't going unnoticed. As I'd expected, she'd denied doing anything, but I didn't believe her. It wasn't like her to let go without a fight and although she'd tried to get Alix to leave me and failed, I knew she likely wasn't done causing hell.

I wished I could go back and never have met the woman, but I couldn't. All I could do was be as supportive of Alix as I could and pray that it would end soon.

Thankfully, I was booked solid and would have other problems to keep my mind busy for the rest of the day.

When I got home that night, Alix had beaten me. She was sitting on the couch staring at a blank television set.

"Precious?" I asked, setting my keys and wallet on the side table as I toed off my shoes.

"Yes?" she asked, shaking her head.

"Why are you just sitting here?" I sat next to her on the couch and wrapped an arm around her shoulders, pulling her close.

"It shouldn't be such a big deal, but I've never felt like someone was so directly targeting me before. It's unnerving and scary," she said into my neck.

I wanted to tell her the more she thought about it the more it took over her thoughts, her life, but I knew it wouldn't help since she was strung so tightly already.

"We'll figure out who it is and make it stop. I promise. I'm working on figuring out who would do such a thing." If she hadn't figured Mariah out as the person behind it, I didn't want to be the one to put the idea in her head. "In the meantime, go to the bedroom and strip."

"John…" She trailed off.

I could tell she wasn't in the mood tonight, but it would help. After working all day I was just as ready for bed as she was, but a little play would help relax her so she'd be able to sleep.

"Precious," I said with a sterner tone.

She sighed and pushed off the couch before trudging down the hallway.

I followed close on her heels and stood in the doorway to watch as she swiftly dropped her clothes into the pile of dry cleaning before climbing onto the bed. Once she was resting on her back, I stepped into the room. Running my hand over the words over her abdomen, I asked, "How did it feel having these words on you all day?"

"Good, sir," she answered, closing her eyes.

"Did you like being so clearly marked as mine where others couldn't see? Did it turn you on to know they couldn't see something so boldly written on you?" I asked, tracing the letters with my finger-tips. "What do you think they'd say if they knew it was there?"

"I loved it. It gave me a sense of calm that even your pearls can't give me. I liked that they couldn't see it. It was personal and sexy, just like what we have between us." She gasped and writhed on the sheets as my fingers dipped between her thighs to drag over her pussy lips.

"I want to watch you play with yourself," I said, stepping back from the bed.

She groaned at the loss of contact, but didn't hesitate to replace my fingers with her own. She didn't take her time and go slowly, but pushed two fingers deep before sliding them back out. Not wasting time at all, she plunged her fingers in again so hard her breasts jiggled. Soon her whole body was nearly sliding up and down the bed with how fast she was fucking herself.

As her breathing sped up and her muscles started to tense, I grabbed her wrist, making her stop.

"No. I didn't say you could come," I told her with a smile.

She groaned and bucked her hips into the air in frustration.

After a minute I released her. I threaded our fingers together and plunged two of my own in along with hers.

Alix cried out and arched against the bed.

"Yes. Please, more," she begged. Bending her legs, she planted her feet on the bed to get more leverage to ride our joined fingers.

I brought her to the edge again before pulling her hand away.

"Damn it!" she shouted and slapped a hand against the mattress.

I flipped her over in a second and slapped her ass hard with my palm before rolling her back over.

"Don't swear or yell at me or I'll make it worse," I said, soothing a hand up her stomach to cup a breast. I let each finger slide over her pert nipple before pinching it between my fingers. "Understand?"

"Yes, sir," she managed to gasp between sucking air into her lungs.

"Start again," I demanded.

She moved her hand back to her pussy and slowly pushed her fingers in and out.

"Did I say you could slow down? You are the one who started fast and hard, keep that pace." I tweaked her nipple for emphasis.

Groaning, she sped up and I stepped back to watch her push herself to the edge.

She'd caught onto the game I was playing and was trying to make it easier on herself. Which was exactly why I forced her to make it harder – it was what she expected from me. It was my job as her dom to push her.

I let her bring herself to the tip, almost to orgasm before stopping her. Over and over again. Each time she got more and more frustrated to be kept from falling over into bliss.

"Again," I told her finally. Before she could touch herself, I added, "You have thirty seconds to get off or you'll have to go all night without it."

It took her twenty-two seconds.

"John!" she wailed as she thrashed on the bed, endorphins ricocheting through her body.

I stripped before climbing between her thighs and sinking into her still-spasming pussy. Her warmth surrounded me and nearly made me come. As much as orgasm denial was hard for her, it turned me on so much I nearly got off from it. Add in her soaking-wet heat squeezing me tight and I was there, but I fought to hold it off.

"Yes! You feel so good," Alix moaned, wrapping her legs around me, pulling me deeper into her.

"Yeah? You like that big cock stretching you? Sliding into while you're still coming?" I lowered myself to my elbows so I could grab handfuls of her hair as I fucked her into the mattress.

"God, yes," she whispered hoarsely. "It'd be even better if you come all over me or fill me and then plug me and keep your come inside me all night."

Christ, I had to stop for a moment at her words. Her words alone could've made me come. She knew exactly what I liked. I hadn't plugged her after coming in a while, but she clearly still remembered.

Once I got myself back under control, I started moving again, then stopped and pulled out.

"Roll over."

She did as I instructed, raising her ass while keeping her chest on the bed.

Instead of spreading her legs, I kneeled on the outside of them and with a hand on her lower back forced her to lean forward until her stomach was barely off the bed. Then I aligned my cock with her entrance and sank deep again. I thrust hard enough that it forced her all the way down onto the bed.

The new position allowed me so deep into her at a new angle we groaned in unison. I kissed along her shoulder until I got to the column of her neck. Sucking hard, I left a bruise on her skin as a reminder of who owned her.

While I enjoyed getting deeper, it also took away the last of my control and I rutted against her hungrily, chasing my orgasm as she moaned louder and louder with her own growing closer with every thrust of my hips.

"Oh... I'm going... to..." Alix grew tense under me as a long, low sound left her lips and her pussy clamped even harder around me.

"Shit. Yes," I barked out harshly as come was yanked out of my dick to shoot deep into Alix. I continued to buck against her as strand after strand left me. It felt like it would never end and by the time my cock stopped spasming, my balls hurt.

"Wow," Alix breathed softly beneath me.

I started to move off her since I was fully lying on her, but she grabbed my hands and instead brought me closer with my arms wrapped around her.

"I love having you so close," she said.

"I love you," I said nuzzling my face into her hair.

"I love you more."

That just wasn't possible, but I let her think what she wanted to.

Chapter Five

~Alix~

A week passed in the hell I'd come to refer to as work. While I was John's submissive, I'd never felt so out of control and in need of someone to take care of me as I had since all my clients were jumping ship. John had been so great about taking care of me and doing his best to support me in every way possible, but every day my guilt grew for being so dependent upon him

I felt like I was taking away time that he should've spent with his clients and taking care of his own business instead of holding my hand while I had numerous panic attacks. Finally I decided I needed to stop, so when I felt a panic attack coming on while at work, instead of calling him, I pulled up a website I hadn't used in over six months.

Once I requested to be connected to a counselor, it took a few minutes before I was surprisingly connected to the same one I seemed to always get.

Counselor21: Well, hello. Been a long time.

BadKitty2: Yes, things had been going so well.

Counselor21: But they aren't any longer? What has changed?

BadKitty2: Trouble at work.

Counselor21: Does this have to do with your addiction?

BadKitty2: ...

Counselor21: Well, let me ask you this then. In the time that you have been away, have you had compulsions to masturbate?

BadKitty2: No. Well, yes, but I've not acted on them.

Counselor21: And now?

BadKitty2: They've gotten worse. I haven't given in, but there are times when I don't think I'll be able to stop myself.

Counselor21: And have you given in at all? Even once?

BadKitty2: ...

BadKitty2: Yes.

Counselor21: Have these times been at work? Or with the man you are seeing?

BadKitty2: The times I've done it with my partner wasn't compulsion. It was... different. The times that felt like I had no control over it were at work when the stress was the worst.

Counselor21: Have you admitted your addiction to the man you are seeing? Or the fact that you are struggling with it again recently?

BadKitty2: Uh... I don't think I've told him straight out, but I think he knows I have some... issues. We have a very... complex relationship.

Counselor21: How do you think he'd take knowing you are giving into you addiction even if he didn't previously know about it?

BadKitty2: Not well. He simply wouldn't be happy about the fact that I was touching myself since he's told me not to without his permission before. Add in that it's something I normally struggle with and I'm sure he'd blow his lid over it.

Counselor21: Permission? Does he control you?

BadKitty2: ...

BadKitty2: Not in any way I don't want him to. He's the biggest reason I've gotten such a good hold on everything. While he controls certain aspects of our relationship, he also helps me become a stronger woman.

Counselor21: Are you happy?

BadKitty2: Of course.

Counselor21: As long as you are happy, then I can't see anything wrong if it is helping you beat your addiction.

Counselor21: Now back to how this conversation started. The anxiety and stress of your job seems to be triggering you. Is it possible to quit or find a new job?

BadKitty2: Are those really the only two options? That's the same things my boyfriend says. I'd like to think I can see it through and turn things around.

Counselor21: But is the harm it causes you personally worth it? It's not your own business, yes? So leaving for another job that isn't triggering you might be for the best.

BadKitty2: No, it's not my business, but it is a job that I've put a lot into and leaving just because of this small thing seems... petty. I feel like I need to get thicker skin and tough it out.

Counselor21: It's not petty when it puts your health, both mental and physical in danger. There are things that are more important than being a good employee.

BadKitty2: What about paying bills? Is money not important?

Counselor21: Can your boyfriend not help support you? Even if only temporarily.

BadKitty2: That's not the point.

Counselor21: Maybe it is. Is your pride getting in the way? Are you too proud to accept help from the man who loves you? Are you too proud to admit that you need help? That you can't do everything alone?

BadKitty2: I don't know. That's asking a lot.

Counselor21: Well, maybe that's what you need to be thinking about more than the stress at work.

BadKitty2: Maybe you are right.

I logged off quickly before the counselor could respond. Whoever the counselor was, they only pissed me off. However, I found myself going through the online conversation repeatedly during the day instead of worrying about the cancels and no-shows.

It wasn't until I'd run through it about a dozen times that I realized that I'd never told them I was seeing someone, let alone a man who could provide for me enough to quit my job. They'd pointed out the same things that John always came back to, which was a bit eerie. However, they'd managed to plant the seed more firmly than John ever had that maybe I needed to quit just to get out of the situation that was making me want to masturbate when I hadn't felt that way in over six months.

Shaking off the strange encounter with the counselor, I tried to focus on my job once more, reaching out to customers I'd worked with in the past but who hadn't scheduled an event recently. Thankfully most of the customers that were still scheduled showed up, however, it also meant I had hours between appointments sometimes. I spent the rest of the day cold-calling people and praying it'd help fill some of the emptied spots for the upcoming week. It didn't.

The only good thing that had come out of the talk with the counselor was that it had helped me avoid a meltdown. I was so off-kilter from it that the conversation had distracted me completely from the overwhelming panic.

And it had worked... until I was leaving for the day.

Just as I walked out the door to head over to John's office, I was harshly bumped from behind. I glanced over my shoulder to see who had done it so I could give them a look, but I stumbled and hit the wall with my back when I saw it was Mariah. Leaning against the wall for support, I met her angry glare.

She smiled sickly as she stepped closer, forcing people to swerve around us.

"Well, well. Look who I happened to *bump* into," Mariah said, taking another small step toward me.

Part of me wanted to wither in her anger but knowing that she was slightly psychotic from my previous encounters with her, I simply wanted to make her go away.

"What do you want Mariah?" I asked her calmly.

"You know what I want," she stated matter-of-factly.

"I don't." I scrunched my eyebrows together. Was she still coming after John? He hadn't said she was hanging around, but I couldn't think of any other reason she would be cornering me on the street.

"Yes, you do. He's mine," she hissed, shoving me backwards.

"John? I think it's his choice who he wants to be with. Neither you nor I can make that choice for him," I tried to reason with her.

"If you were out of the picture, he would come back to me," she said, leaning close so that our faces were only inches apart. "Why don't you just leave him?"

"Because I love him." The words were out of my mouth before I even had to think about how to answer.

"I love him more. I can give him what he needs. You can't," she growled.

"How would you know? Are you in the bedroom when we are together?" I asked, trying desperately to keep my own temper under control.

"Trust me. I know and so will everyone else soon enough," she said, and with one final glare she turned and disappeared in the crowds of people moving about on the sidewalk.

I leaned my head back against the wall and sucked in a few deep breaths to regain my composure. The bitch was crazy, no doubt about it. Too bad I didn't know how to get her to move on from John. She unnerved me more than scared me. She didn't seem to get that he didn't want her anymore, or if she did, she simply ignored it.

After a few moments, I pushed off the wall and made my way to John's office. I greeted April, who waved to John's cracked office door letting me know he was expecting me.

Sticking my head in, I slowly opened the door and couldn't help but smile when he looked up expecting to see April, but his face completely changed and a smile of his own spread over his face when he spotted me.

"Precious," he said, rolling his chair back from his desk.

I dropped my purse on his desk and sat in his lap, wrapping my arms around his neck. It was my favorite place to be. In his arms. In his lap. Surrounded by his strength and comforting touch.

"What's wrong?" he asked after a moment.

"Well, I just saw Mariah. Seems she hasn't given up on her mission of getting you back," I said, followed by a long, slow exhale. "You're the psychiatrist — tell me, why is she so crazy?"

"If I knew, I'd happily bring you in on the secret and make her go the hell away." He sighed and held me tighter.

I could easily tell he was as frustrated with the situation as I was.

"Maybe I need to have a little visit with her to get her to see reality," he said even as he shook his head. "However, with her, who knows? It might only egg her on more."

That thought made my insides cramp. I didn't want him and her anywhere together, let alone somewhere private and alone. Not that I doubted him or thought anything would happen, I just didn't like that she'd be getting what she wanted — to see him and have him all to herself for any amount of time.

"Let's go home, Precious," he said, standing and carefully setting me on my feet.

"Are you done for the day?" I asked. I'd only expected to drop in and give him a kiss before going home.

"I am now. I can move patients around. This is more important right now." Clasping my hand in his, he pulled me toward the door as I still tried to protest.

"But... You need to work..." I said as I followed him with halting steps.

He stopped and spun around to face me at the same time he kicked the door closed with his foot.

"Are you pushing me? I said it was time to go." His voice was hard. It was his dom voice and I immediately straightened my shoulders.

"No, sir," I said, bowing my head.

"I think you were. You seem to think that I can't handle the Mariah situation. You don't believe me when I say things will work out at work. I think it is more than time for a punishment for constantly second-guessing me." He took off his suit jacket and placed it on the hook on the back of the door before pocketing his cufflinks. Rolling up his sleeves, he stepped closer to me.

I knew I was indeed in need of a punishment since I had questioned his dominance and tried taking control of situations he said he'd take care of or doubted that he would do as he said. As his submissive, I'd basically spit on his dominance and that wasn't acceptable.

"I'm sorry, sir," I whispered breathily.

"Fine." He shrugged off my apology because we both knew it wouldn't be enough. "Bend over my desk. Drop your skirt before you do so."

I unzipped my bottoms and let them slide down around my ankles, revealing my thigh-highs and garter belt. Then I did as instructed, folding my arms under my head and rested my forehead on them.

"Three for questioning me. Three for not trusting me. One to make sure it sinks in," he said, moving to stand next to me. "Count. Lose count and I'll start all over."

The first slap landed on my left cheek and made me yelp as heat blossomed from the impact.

"One, sir," I said before biting on my lip in anticipation of the next one.

The second one landed on my right cheek and was equally hard and painful, but I managed to contain the sound of pain that wanted to escape.

"Two, sir," I groaned. This was definitely a punishment spanking, not a pleasure one. There was nothing sensual or playful about it. Simply a lesson being taught.

Three and four landed on top of the first two and I counted for him. When the fifth landed over the sore spot that had endured two spankings already I couldn't hold back my scream.

"Five, sir," I gasped as a tear ran down my cheek. This one was harder than the other ones and hurt exponentially more because of the already-heated skin it landed on.

Another one on the opposite side and I cried out again fighting the urge to wiggle my hips in the hope it'd help alleviate the burning pain in my ass.

"Six, sir," I said. Tears flowed freely down both cheeks. I couldn't stop them. The spanking hurt as intended and made me not wish to be punished again anytime soon.

The final blow landed and I nearly collapsed with relief that it was over.

"Seven, sir."

"Good girl. You did very well, Precious," John told me.

Though we'd been together for a while, I'd only ever had a true punishment delivered a handful of times. Even if I enjoyed pain most of the time, the type that came with little to no warm-up and knowing that I had failed my master I tried to avoid at all costs. There was no pleasure in failure and disappointment.

"Get dressed. We are leaving," John said as he rolled his sleeves back down and refastened his cufflinks.

I pulled up my skirt and zipped it. The material that had once felt sexy only aggravated my angry, spanked ass. I grabbed my purse and followed him out of the office.

He stopped to inform April that he would need the rest of his clients for the day rescheduled then and only then did he look at me. Threading his fingers through mine, he led me to the front door and out it without another word.

It was as we walked toward his car that I realized it was very likely that April had heard what had just happened in his office, but she didn't look shocked or even surprised when I'd glanced at her. Apparently she wasn't surprised by the sounds of a spanking being doled out. Perhaps she was in the BDSM lifestyle too. I'd have to ask a few questions the next time I saw her.

Chapter Six

~John~

When we got to my car, I watched as Alix shifted uncomfortably while waiting for me to open the door for her. She sat and continued to shift in an attempt to find a comfortable spot.

"Stop wiggling. I'm sure it hurts to sit on your raw ass, but you'll just have to deal with it," I said coolly. I didn't particularly like knowing she was in pain, but that was part of the punishment. She'd probably have a hard time sitting down not only the rest of the night but also tomorrow while at work. That thought pleased me.

She wiggled once more, then settled into place with her hands folded in her lap.

The drive home was filled with comfortable silence. Once we got to the house, I parked and ran around to open the door for Alix. When she stood, she let out a little gasp and I grinned at her.

"Sore, Precious?" I asked and she nodded. "Go to the bedroom and strip."

Alix walked into the house and I watched her go, enjoying the sight. She was so beautiful and sexy it was almost painful, but I wouldn't have it any other way. Everything about her was perfect.

At a much slower pace, I followed. I stopped to drop my keys and wallet on the shelf by the front door, then toed off my shoes and tugged off my socks before continuing toward the bedroom.

Seeing Alix on her knees with nothing on but my pearl necklace made my cock swell appreciatively.

"Undress me," I ordered as I dropped my socks.

She stood and walked to me. Her delicate hands glided over my stomach up to my chest, dipping under my coat to slowly push it off my arms. Her hands followed the material until it fell off to pool on the floor.

My pulse sped up as her hands moved back up my biceps to stop at the tie I wore.

Pulling tenderly on the material, she loosened it from around my neck before slipping it off. Surprising me, she dropped it around her own head so it draped down between her beautiful breasts.

One button at a time, she unfastened my shirt until she reached my pants. Changing directions, she reached for my wrists so she could undo my cufflinks. Once the first one was free, she surprised me yet again by pinching her own nipple with the it, using it as a makeshift clamp. She repeated it with the other cufflink before she pulled my shirt from my slacks and finished unbuttoning it.

Her palms ghosted up my abdomen, chest and shoulders before moving down my arms. Before my shirt even joined my jacket on the floor, her fingers were tugging at my belt.

I shrugged and wiggled my arms the last bit needed to lose the shirt. I was ready to be as naked as she was. Seeing her use the items I wore daily to work as toys had my cock begging to be released and my palms yearning to be filled with her silky skin.

As soon as my belt was undone, she swiftly unbuttoned and unzipped my pants.

She moaned at the sight of my cock pulsing beneath my cotton briefs. Fishing her hand into them, she pulled my cock out and licked her lips.

"Please, Master, may I taste?" she begged. Her eyes were locked on my cock as she sank to her knees.

"If you insist," I said, biting back a moan of my own. It turned me on to know she was as needy as I was. All thought fled the instant her lips locked around the head of my dick. My hips jerked forward on their own and my head dropped back before I regained control. I looked down and watched her bob slowly down my length, then back up again.

I should've been upset with her taking the reins by using my cufflinks and tie, but I was also excited by her showing me that she didn't want to wait to find the actual toys. While the material hung uselessly around her neck for now, I knew she'd put it on so I could use it when we had sex to direct or even choke her if I felt the desire to do so.

Just as I felt my balls pull up and was going to tell her to stop, I heard her phone ringing in the other room.

She paused for a moment, then started sucking me deep again. However, when the chimes stopped only to start up again, she let my cock slide from her lips.

"Sir, can I get that? It might be work," she asked.

I wanted to say no. I wanted to tell her to get on the bed so I could fuck her. Instead, I said, "Be quick."

"Thank you, sir," she said before running from the room.

I sighed. Even if it was her job, I didn't care for the interruption, but I knew that her job was important to her, and with everything else that had been going on I knew she'd be distracted until she knew what the call was about.

Stepping out of my pants and underwear, I walked after her, completely nude. She was standing near the door looking like a fucking wet dream, still in my tie and cufflinks, while she held her phone up to her ear.

"Is it work?" I mouthed and she shook her head. That made me smile. I didn't care who else was on the phone. Moving behind her, I pulled her flush to my front. My cock slid between her cheeks and she laid her head back against me. I could hear a voice on the other end of the phone, but not what they were saying.

Alix made noncommittal sounds to whatever they were saying even as she rubbed her ass along my cock.

I pressed my mouth to her other ear.

"Don't make a sound," I breathed quietly. She nodded hesitantly.

Sliding one hand around her hips, I dipped it between her thighs to tickle along the delicate flesh there. My other hand wrapped around to squeeze one of her breasts and support her as I plunged two fingers into her.

Her breathing sped up, but she didn't make any other indication even as I felt her tense slightly at the intrusion.

My fingers pulled out only to press back into her as my thumb rubbed along her clit teasingly. Having gotten her off with my fingers more times than I could count, I knew exactly where her sweet spots were. I found the sensitive spot inside her and rubbed my fingers along it each time they filled her and again as they slid back out.

Alix was trying to pay attention to the phone call and what I was doing at the same time. Her responses to the caller got fewer and fewer as her pussy got wetter and wetter.

"Don't forget you are on the phone," I reminded her before dragging my tongue along the column of her neck.

She said something to the person, but I wasn't paying attention. I was more focused on getting her off before she got off... the phone, that is.

Suddenly, her entire body tensed and vibrated in my arms. I tightened my hold on her and slowed my fingers so I could milk out her release for as long as possible. Eventually she sighed and then said something brief into the phone before hanging up.

"That was evil. We're both probably going to hell now," she said before laughing half-heartedly.

"If the other things I've done haven't gotten me on that list already I don't think what we just did will," I said shrugging. "Who was it, anyway?"

"Some church."

Her response made me pull back from her.

"I'm sorry?" I sputtered.

"A church. Apparently I am in need of saving from the evils I participate in and they would be happy to come over to have a sit-down chat about all the ways I need to turn my life around. They can save me from myself, supposedly," she said, and I could see all the tension I'd worked to relieve her of come right back.

"What the fuck?" I snapped.

"Yeah, that's about what I was thinking." She turned in my arms to face me. "I don't know how the hell they got my number or what they think I'm doing, but it was... weird. However, you made it much more interesting. So I guess I owe you a thank you."

"I can think of one way you can thank me," I said, smirking and glancing down at my hard, dripping cock.

"Mmm, my favorite way to say thank you." She smiled, but it was still tight.

"On the bed, now," I told her.

In the bedroom, I watched as she climbed onto the bed and spread her legs, arms over her head.

"Mmmmm." I dragged out the sound while taking in every inch of her exposed skin. My cock was begging for attention so I wrapped my hand around it and slid it slowly down the hard shaft. Stepping closer, I licked my lips as my eyes continued to consume the luscious woman sprawled out before me. Mine. She was all mine.

Her nipples were dark red from the cufflinks still clipped to their tips. I wanted to bite them and turn them purple under my touch, but decided against it.

Still moving my palm over my dick, I walked around the bed as if one side of her was better than the other. It wasn't. Both were equally tantalizing. All I had to do was pick where I wanted to start devouring her. Moving to kneel on the bed next to her, I tugged on one cufflink, making Alix cry out and arch up off the bed. I smirked and adjusted my knees so one was on either side of her shoulders. Leaning forward, I grabbed onto the headboard with one hand while guiding my cock to her lips with the other.

"Take it. Take all of me, Precious," I demanded and she did so without hesitation, sucking me to the back of her throat. Deep enough that she gagged around me, but didn't pull back for a few seconds. She clamped her lips tight around the crown and sucked hard on it, tearing a gasp from my own mouth.

I dropped my hand to her hair and balled it in my fist as she started to bob up and down my length in earnest.

"God, yes. Show that dick all your love. Worship it with everything you have," I groaned. I didn't have to tell her to do any of it, she already was, but the words were automatic, part of me that I couldn't hold back.

She slithered a hand down to cup my balls gently, only adding to the maddening desire building within me. Her delicate fingers slipped behind my tight sack to nudge against my perineum in time to her sucking down my cock like it was the best thing she'd ever tasted.

My dick pulsed as a small stream of precome escaped. She knew all my buttons and pressed them with a precision that drove me to the brink in minutes. I hated how easily she could get me there while at the same time loving that she paid so much attention to my body each and every time we were together.

I had to pull out of her glorious lips or I'd end up coming too soon. She pouted when it popped out and I moved out of reach.

"Sir..." she pleaded while her hips gyrated on the bed. "I wasn't done."

I wanted to spank her for that alone. She knew I was in control and she'd pushed me enough. It was sexy at times, but when I said enough, that was the end. No questions or begging would change my mind. She knew this. Deep inside, I knew she needed me to push her to help her vacate her own thoughts. Once again, she knew how to show me exactly what she needed without needing to say it outright.

I scooted down the bed so I could take one of her nipples into my mouth and tugged on the turgid peak with my teeth.

She screamed and bucked under me, but didn't truly try to get away or say her safe word. I'd never heard it out of her mouth and didn't anticipate that I would.

Releasing her, I moved lower, dropping kisses as I went. I sucked a mouthful of her fragrant skin into my mouth and made sure to use enough pressure that it would leave a mark on her stomach when I released it. Then I continued to move down again until I found the apex of her legs. I kissed between her hipbones, then down the crease where they met her thighs. Jumping across her weeping center, I kissed up the other side until I was back at the hip bone I'd started with.

She groaned and fisted her hands in the blankets over her head.

I knew what she wanted. I wanted the same thing — to be buried in that beautiful pussy. It wasn't time yet for that. Teasing was half the fun. Watching her pussy lips get plump and full while her juices slowly grew enough to make them glisten was the goal for this little game. Getting her turned on so much she didn't think she could handle any more teasing. Of couse, she could and I would show her that. Then I would make her come all over my face, fingers, and cock. Come until she couldn't remember her name, let alone the shit going on at work or the stupid phone call she'd just taken. Those were things for me to worry about and deal with.

Ghosting my fingertips over the path that my lips made just taken had her gyrate in the hope of getting my fingers where she wanted them. I smiled against the soft flesh of her thigh.

"Please, Master," she begged. "Touch me. Fuck me. Fill me. I need you. I need to come. Master, please."

Now that was what I wanted to hear her say. I wanted her on edge, not topping from the bottom or trying to tell me what was coming next in a roundabout fashion.

"What was that? I *am* touching you. Don't you feel my fingers?" I asked, barely touching the crease between her thigh and pussy. There was a light sheen to her pussy lips. Yeah, she was more than turned on. Fuck, the sight made my mouth water. "Is that not enough?"

"No, sir. I need mo..." Her words trailed off in a gasp because I'd plunged two fingers between that beautiful, glistening flesh. "Yes! Yes"

"Mmm. Better?" I asked, kissing the top of her mound briefly.

"Y...Yes, sir," she stuttered as a ful-body shudder ran through her.

My fingers continued to glide in and out of her. The sound of them squishing around in her arousal filled the room and her scent surrounded me. I couldn't hold back any longer and buried my face, moving it side to side to get deep into her pussy so I could suck her clit into my mouth. Pulling back, I let it pop out so I could lap at all of her while still fucking her.

"So delicious," I whispered reverently. It didn't matter if she heard me or not. It was the truth. I dove back in to flick her clit rapidly with the tip of my tongue. My hips moved on their own to buck against the bedding for friction against my rock-hard cock. My control was cracking and I'd have to fuck her before long, but I fought to hold onto it for as long as I could.

"Oh... Oh, yes... Sir!" Alix gasped and rocked against my invasion. Her tightening pussy told me she was so close.

I thrust into her a couple more times while teasing her clit before pulling my fingers from her and licking her clean. Then I sat up on the bed, resting on my knees, while looking down at her.

Her creamy skin was molten with red spots as her chest rose and fell rapidly.

"Christ," I breathed and stroked my dick a few times. Precome was leaking freely from the tip. I was too turned on for it not to be. Just looking at Alix like that could've sent me over the edge, but I wanted to be deep in her when that happened. I hooked her knees over my arms and opened her up even more for me before she reached down and lined me up. With one strong thrust of my hips, I was deep in that snug, hot cavern created just for me. My own personal heaven. It felt so fucking perfect I had to stop a moment to appreciate it.

"Master. Sir. John!" Alix moaned and pushed down on me.

It broke the last shred of control I had been trying to hold onto. My hips snapped back, then slammed forward to fill her once again. All I could do was watch her beautiful face, her lips open as she gasped for air, her tits jiggling from the force of my fucking. A thin layer of sweat coated her entire body as she constantly made mewling noises of pleasure.

"Precious. I love fucking you. I love looking at you. I just fucking love everything about you." Words were pouring out of my mouth uncensored and I could do nothing to stop them, as my body had taken over and I was lost in her completely. She owned every part of me and I had no idea how to let her know. It was about so much more than sex, although I couldn't focus on anything other than her body's tight grip around mine at that moment.

I dropped Alix's legs and fell forward so my weight pressed her into the bed. Resting on one elbow, I flipped open one of the cufflinks, releasing a nipple then did the same to the other. Alix screamed, body tense, and arched sharply off the bed when her release finally found her, even though I was much heavier than her. I kept pounding into her until she relaxed and then pulled out from her still-quivering pussy. Shuffling up the bed, I kneeled over her chest and roughly yanked on my dick. My balls tightened when Alix opened her mouth and stuck out her tongue even as she still struggled to come down from her orgasm.

Finally, I couldn't hold back anymore and my come spurted out in thick ropes across Alix's face one after another as my hips jerked, shoving my cock through my fist. I nearly fell face-down on top of Alix, but grabbed the headboard with the hand not covered in spunk as I breathed harshly. All of my muscles shook with the amount of energy they'd exerted during the fuck, exactly the way I loved to feel.

I jumped when a warm, wet mouth surrounded my rapidly-softening cock, sucking off the last of my release. Without even opening my eyes that I hadn't realized I'd closed, I knew Alix was smiling.

She carefully took my hand from around myself and licked it clean as well. It wasn't something she did often, but I loved when she took all of me even when she didn't have to.

When I got my breathing back under control, I moved down in the bed to lie next to her. There were still strands of come on her face and I smiled at her. She'd cleaned me, but left what was on her face.

"Do it," she whispered, meeting my gaze.

With my thumb, I spread the creamy substance into her flesh. I smoothed it out until it started to dry. When I started to climb from the bed, she wrapped a leg around mine to stop me.

"I love you too. Even all your quirks," she said with a soft smile on her face. The smile I'd been dying to see since she'd walked into my office earlier. "Especially because you feel so protective of me and like to mark me. It's so sexy."

"You are so sexy and I love you too. Now let's get you cleaned up so we can go find something to eat," I said, placing a chaste kiss on her swollen lips.

"I thought you already did that." She giggled and I couldn't help but wrap her in my arms for a deeper kiss.

I'd missed this side of her. The side that was relaxed and joked around. It was refreshing and reassuring to see it again.

"You are the most precious thing in the whole world to me," I said, feeling my face burn. I never blushed, but apparently sharing such intimate thoughts brought out the teeniest part of me that was still able to be embarrassed.

"And you are the same to me," she replied, snuggling into my chest and completely missing my undoubtedly red cheeks.

Chapter Seven

~Alix~

I watched as John walked back to the bathroom with the washcloth he'd used to clean my face in his hand. The man had the most perfect ass I'd ever seen. Then again, that'd been one of the first things I'd noticed about him, even when he had been fully dressed. So tight and muscular. I had no doubts about how it got that way. My entire body still throbbed from his recent throw-down.

When he walked back into the room, I watched his flaccid dick swing with his steps as his muscular thighs bunched and relaxed. He walked over to me and wrapped the tie still around my neck around his hand. Tugging slightly on it, he forced me to sit up until he could kiss me tenderly.

"Come, Precious. Keep looking at me like that and we'll never get food." His voice was stern, but he smiled, letting me know he appreciated me looking at him.

I climbed from the bed and followed behind him as he led me with the tie to the kitchen. As much as I loved the pearl strands he used as his collar to let me and everyone know I was taken, I liked the much sturdier material of the tie. He could control me much better and not worry about breaking the delicate necklaces. I had over a dozen of them that he'd gifted me with. Always pearls. Always top of the line. Always expensive.

"Sit," he instructed me, pointing to the counter.

I could've hopped up on my own, but waited for him to put his hands on my waist and help me onto the ice-cold marble slab. I shivered, since being completely nude didn't offer much against the chill, but I wasn't going to complain because it also felt wonderful against my still-burning ass.

As much as it had hurt when he'd given me the punishment in his office, it had only made me fly higher and get off that much harder when we'd gotten home.

When I glanced at the clock, I was surprised that more than two hours had passed since I'd left work. Guess it's true what they say, times flies when you are having fun. I smiled at the thought and John tilted his head in question when he caught it as he retrieved items from the fridge for dinner.

"Just feels good to be relaxed for once," I told him as I leaned back on my hands.

"It's nice to see you smiling again," he said, smiling back. He went back to preparing the meal and I couldn't help but watch.

I'd never met a man who was so comfortable naked as he was. It was rubbing off on me. Before all the work drama had started, it wasn't unusual for us to both be in the kitchen just like this since we'd usually end up ravishing each other as soon as the other one arrived. How quickly that had changed, and I missed it.

My phone started ringing and John put a hand on my knee to stop me from jumping down to get it.

"Leave it. At least until after dinner. Please?" he asked. He rarely asked anything of me so I simply nodded and tried to ignore the loud chimes.

It wasn't until then that I realized that as stressed as I was, he too was carrying that stress. Not just because I was relying upon him and constantly coming to him for support, but simply because I was upset, he was too. And that had me falling just a bit more in love with him than I already was, which I didn't think was possible.

John was mixing things in a skillet on the stove when he suddenly dropped the spoon he'd been using and spun on me.

I looked at him surprise, wondering what had happened. I was about to break the silence when he moved between my thighs, spreading them wide enough to accommodate his hips.

"Marry me," he said, staring straight into my eyes.

I sputtered and had to force myself to close my gaping mouth.

"Uh…" I got stuck on the single word. It was absolutely the last thing I'd expected him to say. Sure I'd thought of possibly getting married, but this wasn't the proposal I'd imagined.

John slid his hands up my thighs until he gripped my hips, then pulled me closer to him until we were flush against each other.

"Make me the luckiest bastard in the world. Marry me, Precious. I know I can't live a single day without you in my life. I won't survive without you. I'll do anything for you. You mean the world to me and I can think of nothing that shows you that like offering you a permanent place in my life that no one else will ever have. You are the only woman to ever touch my heart and no one else ever will. You didn't just touch it, you came in and stole the whole damn thing. I am all yours in every possible way. Tell me that you feel the same. Tell me you'll give me the chance to spend the rest of my life trying to show you just how precious and treasured you are. You don't have to answer me now. I don't even have a ring. I wasn't exactly planning this." He paused for a breath, but didn't give me a chance to say anything before continuing. "I want you. There is nothing more in the world I want. I'll do this right if you want. I'll get a ring and get down on one knee somewhere super-romantic. I just want you to consider giving yourself to me for the rest of our lives."

I waited to make sure he was finished and when he didn't start up again, I took his face in my hands and smiled.

"I would love to be your wife. I don't think there is any other situation that would fit us better than this." I smirked as I glanced down at my still-bright red nipples and his tie that hung between my breasts. When I looked back up, I was startled to find a sheen over his eyes. "What? What's wrong?"

"Say it again," he said. His voice broke in a way I'd never heard before.

"I want nothing more in this world than to be your wife," I said, understanding what had moved him so much.

His lips crashed to mine as he pulled me even closer, crushing me against him. Again and again his lips moved over mine, but not in a heated way, more like they were saying thank you for him.

Finally, he pulled back and pressed his face into my neck. I rubbed his back as I felt him shake. Long minutes passed before he managed to pull free again. Immediately he turned his back to me.

I jumped off the counter and slipped between him and the stove. Clasping his face in my hands again, I forced him to look at me. I wiped my thumbs over the tears that rolled down his cheeks.

"Don't hide them from me," I whispered. "They are happy tears, right?"

"Yes, absolutely." He shook his head softly as if there wasn't anything else they could be. "Sorry..."

I cut him off.

"Did you think I'd say no?" I asked, trying not to sound inconsiderate, but confused.

"I don't know. I hadn't thought that far ahead." He took a deep breath and let it out slowly. "I can't express how I feel right now. It's like I've been freed after living in this cage I didn't even realize was there."

I smiled brightly at him. That I understood. The knowledge that everything you were feeling for someone was reciprocated did amazing things to a person.

"How about we go shopping for rings and grab something to eat while we're out?" I suggested, figuring some fresh air would be a good thing for both of us after such a heavy conversation. Plus, if I was honest, I wanted his ring on my finger sooner rather than later. What woman wouldn't? I wanted to show the whole world that not only was he mine in the BDSM community, but everywhere, in every way.

"Only if we can come back and consummate our engagement," he said with a completely serious look on his face.

"Oh I don't know how a girl could say no to that." I laughed and moved out of his reach, because I knew if he put his hands on me now we'd end up in bed again. Right now I just wanted to look at wedding rings for the first time in my life, while ignoring that dark cloud that was hanging not far off for a little while longer.

***

We searched in two ring stores for a few hours, but there wasn't anything I thought was fitting for not just me, but our relationship. Then we grabbed something to eat before returning home where John made sweet, slow love to me.

Weeks passed as we continued to hunt for the perfect ring; clients still cancelled while new clients continued to ask for unusual and kinky events that I had to turn down, and my phone rang at least once an hour with one church or another telling me they could save my soul. Eventually I started blocking their numbers, but they always seemed to find a new phone to call me from. I wanted to throw my phone out the window, but I needed it in case work needed me, a client needed to change something at the last minute, and, of course, as a constant tie to John.

After setting up for a big event and making sure all the caterers had what they needed, my boss called me into her office.

I sat in one of the uncomfortable, but modern-looking chairs on the other side of her desk.

"Alix," she began. "You have been a wonderful asset to this company since you were hired. That is, until recently. I have been in touch with numerous of your previous clients who have taken their business to other facilities. What I found out disturbed me."

"What did they tell you?" I asked. I wanted to know what was happening as much as anyone.

"That you are participating in life-threatening behaviors with this new man you are dating..."

I cut her off before she could continue.

"What I do outside of work in no way affects how I do my job. Not that it is really anyone's business, but it's not life-threatening to myself or anyone else," I said defensively.

"Not only that, but that you are using your office, the public restrooms, as well as who knows where else as places to do things that should only be conducted in private." She kept talking as if I hadn't spoken.

I stared at her with my mouth hanging open. There was nothing I could say to dispute that. However, I didn't think there was any proof of it.

"And while that alone is enough to fire you, I must say the part that really was the final straw was that I've heard you are now telling the people at these so-called events you go to that they can use our hotel for their disgusting get-togethers. You have sullied our reputation in such a way that I don't know if we will recover from it. The first thing to be done though is to fire the person responsible, which is you. I hope you understand that you will not be getting a recommendation from us." She stood and motioned toward the door.

I knew there was nothing I could say to save my job. Not only would there not be a recommendation for my next job, but it'd also be highly unlikely I'd be offered any other job in the field when word got around what had happened.

Tears burned in my eyes as I walked swiftly to my office, my former boss right behind me. I gathered the few belongings I had and stuffed them in my purse before heading for the main door. Jennifer called out to me from the front desk, but I shook my head, keeping my eyes on the ground.

Once outside, I turned and ran in the opposite direction from John's office. I wanted to go to him. I wanted the comfort he could offer, but I couldn't do it. Even knowing that it was coming, I wanted to lash out at the world. It wasn't fair. Yes, some of what I was being accused of was truth, but I hadn't done it in months, almost a year, so it felt like a kick to the gut to have it brought up now.

Never had I thought being part of the BDSM scene as life-threatening or job-affecting. Then again, it didn't matter what I thought, did it? The job I loved, the job I'd worked so hard at, was gone.

Sometime later, I found myself sitting on a bench in a park. I didn't know where I was. It didn't matter. I didn't care. While I knew I should at least call John, I didn't. He wouldn't understand. His job was secure. He didn't have to worry about how he was going to pay bills or buy food. I knew he'd take care of me, but that wasn't the woman I was. I *needed* to take care of myself. Could I let someone else have that much control of me? I'd rely upon him. I'd be stuck if I ever decided I didn't want to be there. There'd be no way for me to leave, no way for me to get my feet back under me now.

I couldn't find a job in the only field I'd worked in during my adult life. Not that I wanted to leave him, but there was always that nagging "what if" in the back of my mind. It wasn't just me that I had to think about either. What if *he* changed his mind about *me*? Then where would I be?

The world was crashing down around me and I couldn't seem to pull two solid, positive things together.

A warm body sat next to me on the bench, but I ignored it until the person slid an arm around my shoulders to give me a side hug.

Looking up, I saw a face I never wanted to have that close to me. Ever. I jumped off the bench and looked down at Mariah.

"What are you doing here?" I asked as tears still streamed down my face.

"I was just trying to comfort you. You looked like you were having a bad day," she said, holding up her hands innocently. "I was trying to be nice."

"Whatever. I don't believe you. All you've ever tried to do is take John away from me." I scowled at her as my tears dried up.

She let out a long sigh and ran a hand through her hair.

"Okay. That wasn't exactly the most brilliant thing I've ever done. I'm not here for John. I went and got some help after all that mess. I've left you both alone since then, haven't I? I was dealing with a lot back then and I'm a different person now. Honest." She lowered both her hands to her lap and gave me what seemed to be a genuine smile. "I'm very sorry about all that stuff. Really. It's embarrassing that I lost it so badly and you both had to deal with the fall-out. I was actually coming to talk to you, to apologize, when I saw you run out of the hotel. I followed to make sure you were okay."

I stared at her for a long moment before huffing and sitting down. I didn't fully believe her, not after all her crazy antics before.

She continued to spout apologies and regrets about everything she'd done, but I only half-listened until she stood and placed a hand on my shoulder.

"Look, I understand if you never want to see me again, but I'd really like for us to at least be able to be friends at some point. John is a great guy and he deserves someone who can make him happy. I know it won't be me and I've come to terms with that. I'm actually dating this really sweet man right now. It's long-distance, but it's gone really well the last few months." She removed her hand and stepped back. "Please, if you ever want to talk, about anything, call me."

She set down a sheet of paper with her phone number on the bench next to me and walked away.

I watched her go in surprise. She seemed very different than the psychotic woman she had been the last time I'd seen her. I still didn't trust her, but tucked the number into my purse anyway.

Talking to Mariah, or rather, listening to her, had helped me calm down and I pulled my phone out. I had a dozen missed calls. Most were from numbers I didn't recognize, meaning they were likely from my new stalkers — I mean, church members. There were two from John though, and I dialed his number.

"Alix?" John answered on the first ring, worry obvious in his voice. "Where are you, Precious? Jennifer called and told me that you were escorted out by your boss and that you looked very upset."

"I'm at some park," I said, not caring to talk about it over the phone.

"Okay... What park?" he asked and I heard him shuffling things around on his end of the line.

"I don't know. Look, I'm fine. I'm just going to go home and we can talk when you get there," I told him. I didn't much feel up to rehashing it all. What I really wanted to do was fall into bed and stay there for a few days.

"I'd feel better if you'd tell me where you are so I can come get you," John said.

"I already told you I don't know where I am. It's just easier if I get a cab and have them take me to the house." I sighed tiredly. "Just finish with your clients and I'll see you tonight. I love you."

I hung up before he could respond. Putting my phone on silent, I leaned back and looked up at the sky.

Time passed as I sat there watching the clouds float overhead until my neck hurt and I got up from the bench.

Luckily, I was able to catch a cab outside a nearby restaurant as they dropped off a couple. I slid into the back and gave him the address before closing my eyes and rubbing my temples with my fingers. My head was starting to ache and bed was sounding even better.

When the car pulled up, I paid the driver and got out. Before I could even reach the front door, it opened and John stepped out. He looked worried. His tie was pulled down, his hair a mess and a frown marred his beautiful face.

"Hi," I said meekly as we got close.

"Hi," he whispered, pulling me into his arms in a tight hug.

"I'm okay." I pulled on his shoulder until he finally released me.

He stared into my eyes for a long time before finally nodding once.

"Let's go inside," he said, weaving his fingers with mine and leading me through the door.

Chapter Eight

~John~

Every muscle in my body immediately relaxed when I drew Alix into my arms as we sat on the couch. Having her disappear on me had made me nearly go out of my mind. Part of me was happy that now the stress of her job would be gone, but it opened a whole other set of issues we'd have to work our way through. However, the only thing on my mind was comforting her and letting it sink in that she was okay and home with me.

Holding her close, I breathed in her scent as much as I could without letting her know. I'd never admitted that I'd stalked her before we started seeing each other and I didn't think it was the time, or that it would ever be the time, to let her know such a thing. Even though she lived with me and was my fiancée, I still couldn't release the soul-deep need I had to have her as close to me as possible. I had to know everything about her.

I didn't think about her as an addiction anymore, but then again I didn't have to peek in windows or stalk her to find out all the details of her life. She willingly shared them with me. I didn't see it as a problem since I didn't do strange things like smell her underwear or wear her clothes, both of which I'd had to counsel men through in the past. It was about finding someone who could handle being in my life and all that came with it.

From the first time I laid eyes on Alix, I knew she was the one for me. I wasn't lying when I said I couldn't survive without her. There was little doubt in my mind that I would completely lose it if she tried to leave me. Not in a way that I would try to stop her, if that's what she truly

68

wanted, but it would crush me. The thought alone made my eyes burn.

I shook my head to clear away the terrifying idea of anything like that ever happening. For some reason my emotions were on the surface when it came to her lately and I didn't know how to handle it.

When she'd accepted my naked proposal, I'd cried. Like a little kid. How pathetic was that? I couldn't hold back the tears though. It was a moment I'd remember for the rest of my life. By far the best moment in all my time on Earth.

"John?" Alix's voice brought me back to the present. From the tone of her voice it wasn't the first time she'd said it either.

"Yes, Precious?" I asked, looking down to meet her gaze.

"Can we not talk about it today? I just want to sit and watch television or a movie with you and pretend it's just a day that we both happen to have off." She looked away, showing me just how tenuous her grip was on her own emotions.

"Absolutely," I said, planting a kiss on her forehead. "Would you like popcorn and hot chocolate to go with the feature this evening, miss?"

She gave me a wobbly smile and nodded.

After another tender kiss on her forehead, I got up to retrieve her favorite snacks.

"Pick something to watch," I called out from the kitchen.

The sound of buzzing came from her purse on the counter while I waited for the microwave to finish. I fished her phone out and felt my blood pressure sky-rocket when I saw it was an unknown number. I slipped out the back door before hitting the answer button.

"Hello?" I said in a sharp tone.

"Yes, this is Betty from…" a soft, feminine voice started.

"Are you calling from a church of any kind?" I cut her off.

"Why, yes, I am calling as part of..."

"Listen here," I interrupted. "You will stop calling my fiancée. She's asked repeatedly. Now I'm telling you that this will stop or I will file harassment charges."

I was trying to keep a lid on my temper, but after the way the day had gone, it was a struggle. I know the words came out bitter and biting and that's exactly how they were meant. Enough was enough.

"But..." she tried again.

"No. The next time you or anyone from your church calls I will be going down to the police station and filing charges. Do you understand me?"

"Yes. I'm sorry to have upset you so much..."

"You haven't upset me. You've made my fiancée cry for the last time. She didn't ask for you to call her nor is she doing anything that she needs to be saved or redeemed from or anything like that," I snarled. "Go bother someone who might actually care."

I hung up and tucked the phone into my pocket before bracing my hands on the railing around the back porch. Dropping my head down, I took a few deep breaths, trying to calm down so I could go and sit with Alix. It was time for me to be the dom she needed. I'd let the shit go for too long because she wanted to be a strong, independent-woman. She could be strong and independent when she was ready to be, but for now it was my turn to take over until things settled down.

After a final long exhale, I returned to the kitchen and grabbed the rapidly-cooling hot chocolate and popcorn before taking them to the living room.

Alix had curled in a ball, her head on the arm of the couch and fallen asleep.

I set the snacks on the coffee table. Picking up the remote, I turned the television off, then scooped her up from the couch. I carried her to the bedroom and set her on the bed. Carefully, I removed her shoes, then her clothes, leaving on her stockings, garter belt and undergarments then I backed out of the room.

Returning to the living room, I took the popcorn to the trash and the mug to the sink to clean out later. Then I went to my office and went about working on putting together the most perfect proposal for her while she napped. I couldn't simply take her out to dinner and pop the question. No, it had to be something special while being something she wouldn't see coming even though she knew I would be asking again at some point.

A few hours had passed before Alix appeared in my doorway. I was in the middle of an online counseling session I'd picked up as a favor for one of the other counselors. Seeing her there looking sleep-tousled with a drowsy smile on her face, I wanted to close the computer down and take her back to bed for something other than sleeping, but couldn't.

"Hey, Precious," I said, standing and moving around the desk to kiss her.

"What are you doing?" she asked, glancing back at the laptop I had open. Even though she'd been resting, she still looked exhausted. The vibrancy of her personality was gone.

"Just working. I'll be done probably in about thirty minutes or so. Sorry." I wrapped my arms around her hips and pulled her against me. "Then I plan to take you back to bed and make you feel all better."

"It's okay. I'm just going to find something to eat," she said softly, brushing my cheek with her thumb before pulling away.

I stared after her for a long moment before returning to my computer. I'd have to make an excuse as to why I'd been gone so long, but it was killing me to see that my beautiful, bright woman had been broken into this sad, quiet shell of a person.

After making it through the last of the session, I closed the computer and went to see where Alix had gone off to. I found her slouched at the kitchen table with a mug in one hand and an untouched sandwich on a plate in front of her. She was staring at the wall.

"Precious?" I asked. My heart hurt knowing that she was so devastated at the loss of her job. Since she hadn't talked to me about it, I didn't know exactly what had happened, but I wouldn't force the subject. She would open up to me when she was ready to.

She turned her head to look at me; a sad smile pulled at her lips, but I knew she was only attempting it for my benefit.

"Let's go to bed," I said while tugging the chair out from the table. I turned it, clamped both her shoulders and forced her to her feet before scooping her into my arms.

Once I got to the room, I put her on the bed and realized she was still in only her underwear. Apparently, she wasn't the only one with a lot on her mind since that was the only way I hadn't noticed her attire before. I trailed my palms down over her chest, stomach and thighs until I could unhook her garter belt from her stockings, then rolled them down one leg at a time. One item after another, I stripped her until she was bare before me, then did the same to myself.

As I moved toward our armoire filled with toys, I smiled because I had an excellent idea come to me. After gathering the items I needed, I walked back to the bedside with them behind my back so Alix couldn't see them.

"Precious, since you are out of sorts this evening, I am going to help you get back into your mind. I want you to take this time to remember the past and all the things that have happened, but don't dwell on them. Simply remember how strong you've been in the past and keep that in your head and heart. Remember that numerous unexpected things have come and gone and all of it has led you to me so that I can take care of you. I'm not going anywhere, no matter what happens, and you need to remember that foremost. Soon you will be my wife and tied to my life in every way possible. Now, please, sit up so we can begin."

She pushed up while keeping her eyes on mine until I handed her the silken strap I had used numerous times to blindfold her.

"Put it on," I instructed her. While I enjoyed putting it on her myself, I had other objects in my hands for the time being.

Once she put the cloth on, I stepped away to turn the bedside lamp on and the room lights off for better lighting. Setting two of the items on the nightstand, I held the long, soft ostrich feather out.

Trailing just the tip of the feather over her ivory skin, I let it tickle her sensitive spots before doing it once more. I made sure to cover every inch of her with it.

Just from the light contact, she was writhing on the bed in anticipation. She knew there was more to come.

"Hands above your head," I instructed and she moved them up.

Setting aside the feather, I opened a drawer on the bedside table and retrieved leather cuffs, then straddled her chest. My fingers drifted up her under arms, over the inside of her elbow and up her forearm until I snagged one wrist between them. I pulled her arm straight out before wrapping the leather around it. With a twist of my hand, I had the restraint in place. I draped the chain around one of the bedposts before dropping my fingers back to her opposite shoulder to repeat the process.

Once she was held in place, I sat back so my ass rested against her chest. Wrapping a hand around the base of my cock, I rubbed the tip of it all over her face, only avoiding where the blindfold was. When it brushed against her lips, she flicked her tongue out and I slapped her with my cock in retribution.

"I didn't say you could touch my dick," I reprimanded her before bringing my stiff length down to slide over her closed mouth. Precome leaked from the tip and I smeared it into her lips before sliding along her cheeks again. Scooting back on the bed slightly, I stopped when I sat on her upper abdomen. Using my hands, I cupped her breasts and pushed them together so I had a nice, warm, soft channel to push my cock through. My thumbs brushed over her nipples as I thrust my dick in and out of her tits.

After a dozen or so thrusts, I moved off her completely and grabbed one of the toys I'd gotten out earlier. I flicked a finger over the sharply-spiked tips of the Wartenberg wheel. It was a toy I hadn't brought out for some time. Not since before Alix had moved in with me.

I moved to stand at the foot of the bed and gently ran the twelve sharp points over the sole of her foot, which made her squirm, but she didn't make a noise.

"Spread your legs," I said, and she opened them for me.

She was already damp and I licked my bottom lip in anticipation as my cock leaked appreciatively at the sight.

I rolled the wheel up the inside of her calf, then down her thigh with barely any pressure.

"Oh!" Alix gasped and tightened her muscles, telling me she was struggling to stay still.

I smiled wickedly and moved to the other leg to repeat the soft, slow pricks against her sensitive flesh. Once I got to the top of her thigh, I skipped over the crease and all of her delicious parts. She wasn't ready for that yet. Instead, I knelt between her spread legs and wheeled up her abdomen, stopping just short of her breasts. Crossing from one side to the other, I tracked back down until I came to her hip bone, then I went straight up the center, all the way up until I was forced to lean forward on one hand. I traced just below her collarbone, only to curve down and up onto a breast.

Alix moaned and gasped occasionally while flexing and releasing her muscles, but she managed to stay completely still otherwise until I ran the sharp tips over her hardened nipple.

"Sir!" she yelled and pushed her head back into the pillow.

Moving along the underside of her breast with almost no pressure at all, I made my way back up to the other collarbone to repeat the process on her other breast. Only here, I used more pressure when the wheel climbed the hill of her breast, then slowed until the wheel dug in deeper and was more biting than it would've been if it was moving quickly.

Alix let out a long moan as the tips sank into her pretty pink nipple, leaving a path of tiny imprints in its wake.

Lowering the Wartenberg wheel, I quietly set it on the mattress next to her and reached out for the final toy. I managed to grab it without jostling Alix or the bed so she jumped when the leather tip of the crop bit into her thigh.

Sitting back on my knees, I used the edge of the crop to roam over her in a random pattern before bringing it down on her breasts and thighs without warning. While normally I adored seeing Alix's skin red from my hand, I was more interested in the sensitivity brought on by the Wartenberg wheel, so I only placed half a dozen or so blows before tossing it off the bed and retrieving the discarded toy.

I moved farther down on the bed so I was eye-level with her pussy. Using my hands, I pushed her thighs farther apart.

"Mmm, look at you. All wet and ready for me. I can't wait to have you stretched around my dick. Feel you squeeze me so tight I want to fill you with come," I said, not looking away from the tantalizing sight in front of me. I buried my nose between her swollen lips and breathed deep, taking her scent into my lungs. "You smell so good it's intoxicating. I can't get enough."

I had to force myself to back away before I lost it and ate her pussy until my face was covered with her come. No, it wasn't time for that yet.

Shaking my head, I took the wheel in my right hand and traced the crease where her thighs met her pussy.

Alix was making mewling noises, which only turned me on more. Hearing her cries of pleasure were almost as good as getting off myself.

Once I'd gone up and down both sides a few times to prepare her for more, I moved to let the wheel dig into her pussy lips lightly. No need to use too much pressure or it'd hurt too much and all the fun would have to stop. However, there was something hot as hell about seeing the little lines of dots all along the most tender spot on her body, so I pushed down a little harder.

When Alix was breathing so rapidly it was likely she'd pass out and her pussy was dripping wet, I finally set the wheel aside only to dive face first into her.

I licked, sucked, and nibbled on her until she was begging me to let her get off.

"Not yet, Precious," I told her as I gave her pussy one long swipe with my tongue.

"Please. Please. Please, sir. *Please*." She spoke rapidly, but put extra emphasis on the last time she said the word.

"Needy, are we, Precious?" I asked as two of my fingers ghosted along her slit.

"Yes!" She shouted it to make sure I understood.

"Then come whenever you want," I told her. "But…"

"But…" she gasped. "What?"

"That means you don't get to come again tonight," I said and she moaned in displeasure.

"No. No, I don't want that," she answered, shaking her head.

"Oh, but I can make this one so good and you need it so bad," I taunted her.

"I can wait, sir," she said, her voice much firmer than before.

"Very well," I sighed as if it was a disappointment. It was. I loved to keep her on the edge when she knew she wouldn't be getting off for a long time. She normally had so much control over her release that she didn't often orgasm without permission, so it was a treat when she did.

Grabbing hold of the base of my cock, I nudged her opening with it.

"Yesssss." She let the last sound drag out.

I teased her by only letting the head of it push into her before pulling it back out again.

She was growing more and more slick around my dick and it was sucking away my control to know how turned on she was. It was always my undoing. Knowing I was bringing her so much pleasure.

One thrust at a time, I sank deeper into her. It was the most painful and delicious torture to take her so slowly. I wanted to slam into her and make her scream for me, but I also enjoyed feeling her slowly part and stretch to accommodate me inside her tight channel.

"Precious, you are so perfect. That pussy is trying to suck me in like it can't get enough of my dick. So damn wet too," I groaned, because she really was too perfect for me. Lowering myself down onto my elbows, I brought our lips together as I started moving my hips in earnest. Sweat was rolling down my back as I struggled not to lose control while still fucking her good.

Our tongues dueled, sliding against one another in a hurried, hot dance of passion as our bodies slid against each other in the most primal of ways.

We had to separate because we were both struggling to breathe as we edged closer to release. I could feel Alix vibrating against me as she attempted to hold hers back until I told her it was okay.

"Come for me, Precious," I said, locking eyes with her.

Every muscle in her body tightened and she arched so sharply against me that had I been a lesser man she might have bucked me off, but I wasn't and she didn't. A loud, long wail escaped as she clamped down tight around me and a wave of moisture ran down my balls.

I continued thrusting and rolling my hips until she'd caught her breath and was pushing up off the bed, encouraging me to go deeper and harder. Hooking my arms under her knees, I pulled her ass up so I could let loose and really slam into her. At that angle, I couldn't last long. It was exhausting and simply felt good to just drop all pretenses and fuck with everything in me until pleasure tore through me and I spewed into her.

"Shit," I gasped, dropping her legs and collapsing onto my locked arms so I didn't fall on Alix.

"I agree," she said, smiling broadly even though she still had the blindfold on and couldn't see me.

Chapter Nine

~Alix~

I felt useless and was bored out of my mind without a job. The first week had been nice as I'd gotten caught up on all the housework that was constantly put aside because we were always tired after work. However, once all that was done, I found myself pacing the house looking for stuff to do. I'd already applied to a few places, but wasn't holding my breath for any call-backs.

Finally, I decided I'd go for a walk to the nearby pet store to go look at the cats that were always there. Maybe I could convince John we needed a pet. I didn't think he'd go for it, but it gave me something to do for a while.

It was a bit of a walk to the store, but it was nice to be out in the fresh air so I strolled at a casual pace and took in the neighborhood.

I sat and played with the two cats that were in the cages for as long as I could, but once my knees and butt started to protest from the hard floor where I'd knelt and sat to reach through the holes, I decided it was time to head back home.

However, when I walked outside the store I was surprised to see Mariah walking toward the door with a small dog in her arms.

"Oh. Hi there!" she said, surprised but friendly as she waved at me and headed in my direction.

"Uh, hi," I said. She wasn't being weird and it really looked like she hadn't expected to see me, so I reached a hand out to let her dog sniff my fingers. "Who do you have here?"

"This is Fluffy." She laughed as if she found the name as ridiculous as I did, but I only smiled in return. "Do you have a pet?"

"No. Why?"

"Well… you *were* just coming out of a pet store," she said, flicking her eyes to the door she'd seen me exit from.

"Oh. Yeah. I was just playing with the cats in the adoption center," I told her, shrugging.

"So are you going to get a cat?" she asked, readjusting her grip on the dog as it wiggled around.

"Probably not. I was just bored and thought it'd be something fun to do." Boy, I sounded like such a loser. No friends to go out with or anything better to do than play with locked-up cats that I didn't really want to take home.

"Well, if you ever get bored again, we could hang out. I volunteer at the pound just a couple miles from here a few days a week. They'd love more help if you're interested." She shuffled around a bit until she could reach a hand into her purse. She pulled out her phone before scrolling through a few pages and turning it so I could see it. "This is their number and location if you want to look them up on your own. Or you could call me and we can go together one day."

I didn't know that I trusted her enough to give her my phone number or make plans with her, but volunteering did sound like something good to do that'd help pass all the free time I had. Pulling out my own phone, I entered the name and number into my contacts before putting it away.

"Thanks. I'll check them out," I told her.

"Great! Maybe I'll see you around. I have to get Fluffy to the groomer, so I have to go, but it was nice seeing you," she said before taking a step away, then turning to head into the building.

I frowned and continued on my way home. Mariah didn't seem at all like the crazy woman I'd met before. She actually seemed... nice. My mind ran through the encounter over and over as I walked, but no matter how I looked at it, I didn't see how getting me to volunteer would help her get John. Hell, she hadn't even brought him up at all.

Deciding to see if she was full of it, I sat down at the computer and looked up the shelter, and sure enough it was where she had said it would be and the phone number listed on their website was the one she'd had in her phone. I called and asked if they were looking for any help and they were. When I went one step further to ask if "my friend" Mariah helped them, they said they didn't know if it was one and the same, but that there was a woman who helped out with that name.

After agreeing to stop by the next day for more information, I hung up and sat back in the chair.

What a strange turn of events. Maybe she really had gotten help and was over all the nutty behavior. Only time would tell, I guess.

I had to decide if I'd tell John that Mariah would be volunteering at the same place I was thinking of giving my time to. In the end I decided against it, since I was planning on finding out when she'd be there and working around it to not have to see her.

When John arrived home that evening, I felt better than I had in days. While I didn't have a job, I at least had something to do besides sit around on my ass all day. I'd applied to a few more positions as well.

It wasn't until both of us were finishing up dinner that I brought up the volunteering.

"So, I walked to the pet store today," I began.

"Oh yeah? What for?" he asked leaning back in his chair while taking a sip of water.

"I was bored and thought I could go play with the kitties they always have there. Then it made me think that I could do something with my time while I wait for a paying job," I said.

"You want to work at the pet store?" He lifted an eyebrow curiously.

"No. No, I want to volunteer at the shelter. It won't help with the bills, but it will give me something to do. Of course, I wanted to run it by you before I committed to anything or even went to see what it was all about." I didn't want him to feel left out of any life choices since I was his submissive. Plus, it was courteous anyway.

"If that's what you want to do, I'm fine with it. I think it'd be good for you to get out and about a bit so you don't feel so cooped up. As I've said a few times now, don't worry about the money. What days were you thinking of volunteering?" he asked, setting his glass on the table.

"I'm not really sure. Do you have a preference?" I knew he liked having me home on the days he worked so that I could have dinner ready and make his time at home less stressful, but I hadn't really thought about what days would be best except that I wanted to try to avoid Mariah.

"I'll have to get back to you on that. However, I would like to have you free this weekend," he stated before standing and collecting the plates.

"What's this weekend?" I looked at him, curious. He hadn't said anything about plans before.

"It's a surprise, Precious." He winked before disappearing into the kitchen.

I wanted to press. I didn't care for surprises, not really. Okay, I liked them, I just hated waiting for the unveiling.

Together we both did the dishes and cleaned up from the meal before I planted myself on the couch while John went to change. He came back with his laptop.

"You have to work?" I tried not to sound upset, but I wanted to spend the time as just the two of us after he spent all day away from me.

"Just for a little bit. I can go in the office if you'd like. I just thought it'd be nice if I could at least sit in the same room as you."

I pouted when he sat in the armchair instead of next to me like he normally did. It took me a minute to answer him.

"It's okay. I just got spoiled, I guess. Plus, I can never have enough of you so I'll have to learn to share you again," I said. I hadn't realized how much I'd taken him away from work when my own job had put me on edge. Never once had he let me down when I'd needed him there for me in any way. It made me feel incredibly selfish even if I didn't realize it at the time. I just had to learn to be happy with the time he did have for me, and he always made sure there was at least an hour a night that was just me and him outside of the bedroom, plus whatever time we spent rolling around naked together.

"It'll get better. I am still adjusting to having you living here." He gave me a sad smile.

It was true. Apparently, before I moved in with him, he'd worked late into the night going through clients' files and reading up on new articles from various medical journals, as well as being part of online group chats where he talked with other people in his field.

I didn't know a lot about it, but it sounded like a lot of things to juggle to keep up with the changes that were constantly happening in the human psyche, which was vital for his job.

"I know. it's even worse now that I'm here all the time instead of gone sometimes doing my own work stuff," I admitted.

"I like having you here. It's comforting to hear you moving around or simply smelling your perfume when I walk into a room after you have. I just have to figure out how to get everything done in less time so I have more to spend with you," he said.

83

"Well, do your thing. I'm actually kind of tired from my walk today." How sad was that? It showed why I needed to get out more when a short walk wore me out.

I zoned out and got lost in prime time television shows. One rolled into another, then another. Before I knew it I was struggling to keep my eyes open and John was still on his laptop.

Yawning, I stood and stretched my arms over my head.

"I'm gonna get a drink, then go to bed," I informed John, heading for the kitchen.

"Okay…" He nodded absently, obviously drawn into whatever he was working on.

I turned quickly when my bladder screamed out that it needed to be emptied and soon. As I strolled behind John, my eyes naturally went to the screen of his laptop. Things seemed to slow to a snail's pace. I'd expected to see one of the numerous sites I'd seen him looking at before. However, what I saw was the counseling site that I had used many times. Surprised by that, I stumbled and reached out for the back of the chair. My eyes focused on the user names on the screen and my heart stopped when I immediately recognized the counselor's name. Then just as quickly as things seemed to have slowed, they sped back up and John quickly changed screens to an article that looked boring as hell.

I couldn't help but notice the worried expression that flashed across John's face before he hid it away.

"Where are you going? I thought you were going to get a drink?" he asked before turning slightly in the chair to fully look at me.

My brain was spinning trying to comprehend what I'd seen.

"I… I, uh, have to go pee," I sputtered before walking as fast as I could to the bathroom and closing the door. After locking the door, I leaned back against it. My heart thundered in my ears as I struggled to draw in a breath.

Why was he on that site? How was it he was talking to the counselor I always talked to? Was *he* the counselor? No, that couldn't be. It just wasn't possible, but why would he lie and tell me that he was working when he was talking to someone else? Did he need help? Or was he giving it?

All sorts of other questions whirled through my brain faster than I could even fully think them. No matter what the reason or explanation, I couldn't help but feel hurt that he'd been lying about something. It wasn't a white lie. It wasn't a miscommunication. He'd blatantly told me he was working to my face. Is that what he was doing? Was he working for the counseling site?

I had told that person things I'd never told other people. It was supposed to be confidential, but if it had been John all along, he'd led me to tell him things he had no right to know. Not without me knowing it was him. Hell, it'd only been weeks since I'd been on the site needing help with issues that involved him. Had he used it to get me to do things he wanted me to do that weren't necessarily for my benefit, mental or otherwise?

There was a knock on the door, bringing me out of my whirlwind of thoughts.

"Precious, are you okay?" John asked softly. "You've been in there for a while. I just wanted to make sure you didn't fall asleep in there."

"Uh, yeah. Just give me a minute," I said before taking a few deep breaths. Flushing the toilet and then rinsing my hands, I pretended that I'd taken care of business when my bladder was still aching in the back of my mind. I opened the door and gave him a half-hearted smile. "Sorry. I must be sleepier than I realized."

"Come on. Let's get you to bed," he said, wrapping an arm around my shoulders.

I turned in his arms and kissed his cheek.

"It's okay. I can get there on my own. Just finish your work stuff so you aren't up all night with it." How I managed to keep my voice from cracking, I don't know, but I did.

"Are you sure? It won't take long to tuck you in." John gave me a funny look.

"I'll be fine," I said, patting his chest softly before breaking his hold on me and walking away before he could say anything else.

Once in the room, I used our bathroom to finally relieve my bladder, then changed into pajamas before crawling into bed. I put my back to the door and John's side of the bed.

When he finally came to bed, I pretended to be asleep even when he tried to rouse me for sex.

"Not tonight," I murmured sleepily and he let it go.

He eventually fell asleep, and I lay there for another ten minutes to be sure he wouldn't wake up before carefully extricating myself from the bedding and heading back to the living room.

I found his laptop plugged in on the kitchen counter where he normally left it. Opening it, I scanned the desktop. Not once in all the time we'd been together had I gone through anything of his, but I had to know. There were too many questions in my head for me to let it go.

He'd wiped his browser history though, so there was nothing there to ease my mind. I opened the website I'd seen him on and was surprised to find that his username was saved but not his password.

That was all I needed, though. The user name matched the counselor I had talked to every single time I'd gone to the website.

My vision felt like it was blacking out so I backed away before stumbling to the couch and falling into it. I couldn't believe it. He'd been manipulating me all along. He'd been sneaking around behind my back telling me what to do and how to feel about so many things he had no right to be involved in since they often included him.

Hours later, I was still sitting on the couch and John came wandering into the room.

"What are you doing already up?" he asked, hiding a yawn behind his hand as he walked past me and into the kitchen.

I heard the hiss and gurgle of the coffee machine, then a moment later I heard the laptop being shut and a curse.

John came to sit next to me, looking much more awake than he had. He didn't say anything for a long moment and I didn't either, simply kept staring at the blank television screen.

"Well?" I finally broke the tense silence when it was clear he wasn't going to.

"I was going to tell you," he said sounding defeated.

"Tell me what exactly?" I turned to look at him then. Anger and hurt warred with confusion and embarrassment inside me and I didn't know which one was stronger right at that moment.

"Everything," he sighed and ran a hand through his hair.

I jumped off the couch and glared at him.

"You better start talking. I don't even know who you are right now. You've been lying to me, leading me on... or was this all some sick game to you? Did you get your jollies off knowing that the sick little girl addicted to touching herself was coming to you both on and off the computer for help? Using one role to help the other get what they wanted while yanking me around?" Anger was obviously winning out at his unwillingness to talk about it.

"Sit down," he said calmly.

"No." I answered firmly. "You aren't my dom, my master or my fiancée right now. You are a stranger to me."

"Don't say that. Let me explain," he said, finally meeting my eyes again.

"I'm trying to but all you keep doing is avoiding it!" I shouted. My face burned with embarrassment as it all sank in at just how stupid I was. I shook my head and walked away from him. Retreating to the bedroom, I yanked my suitcase out from under the bed and threw open the top.

"What are you doing?" John asked in a bored tone.

"I'm fucking leaving. What does it look like?" I spat. It didn't take me long to have an armful of panties and bras in the bag.

"You aren't going anywhere."

That made me stop and glare at him.

"Why? You going to stop me? Hold me here against my will?" I scoffed and moved past him so I could get my clothes from the closet, but he did stop me.

His hand wrapped around my arm and he spun me so my back hit the wall and he was pressed against my front.

"You. Aren't. Leaving," he said, finally angry.

"You can't stop me," I spat back.

"Watch me."

We stared into each other's eyes for a long time until finally I sighed. I knew I couldn't get out from his grip, nor did I really want to leave. At least not until I got some answers.

"Calmer now?" he asked.

"Yes." I gave a tense nod.

Slowly, his fingers unwound from around my arm as if he didn't completely trust that I wouldn't bolt. He had good reason, because the thought crossed my mind, but everything I owed was there and I would have to come back and deal with him at some point.

"Can we please sit and talk about this?" he asked, nodding toward the bed.

"No. We can go to the living room or the dining room. I'm not getting on the bed with you." I might have calmed down, but I was still plenty angry.

He sighed, then held out a hand toward the door.

We both settled into opposite corners of the couch before he started talking.

"I'm sorry I didn't tell you earlier. It was wrong of me. I didn't realize who you were at first... No... All right, I'm going to come clean about everything and you have to promise me you'll at least hear me out until the end and then you can do as you wish and I'll stay out of your way."

I stared at him hard. He'd just forbidden me from leaving and now he was telling me that he basically knew I'd want to leave once I heard it all. Did it get worse than what I already knew? How would that be possible? Guess I was about to find out.

"Okay. I promise to let you say everything you have to say." I couldn't promise anything other than that until I knew the extent of what it was.

He took a slow, deep breath before blowing it out and running a hand over his face.

"About four months before I met you at The Scene, I'd walked into the hotel I regularly took my clients to. There was this drop-dead beautiful woman there. She'd flashed me a killer smile before turning back to whomever she was talking to. While I knew she'd thought of me as just another customer in the lobby, something inside me clicked. I *had* to know more about this woman. *Everything* about this woman. I did things I'm embarrassed to admit. Things that would probably get me arrested if I'd been caught. However, none of that mattered at the time. I burned to get closer to her, to know her in every sense. While I'd never once in my life had a hard time talking to a woman, I couldn't seem to find it in myself to speak to *this* woman. Then one day out of the blue, this woman looked up at me and locked gazes with me while she did something I never thought I'd see her doing. It turned me on to the point I nearly embarrassed myself right then and there. I had managed to catch her eye somehow. Granted, things took a long time to come to the point where we could be together in a normal relationship.

"Sound familiar? Well, in my exploration of knowing all there was to know about you, I had found your IP address, and when I'd found it was you coming to the counseling site that I worked on sometimes, I set it up so I was the only counselor you could be connected to. I wanted to be the one to support you, the one to help you work through your problems, not some random person who would never be able to relate to you like I did. So, yes, I hid a lot from you, but I never did it to hurt you or embarrass you. To this day, not a single person knows that I talked to you on there or knows any of the things you told me there. Those are my most treasured secrets that I plan to take to the grave. They were given to me in times of duress and when you were the most vulnerable. However, I understand if you are upset about the deception and need time to gather your thoughts without me around." John stopped talking and looked down at his hands, his shoulders curled inward in a way that I'd never seen on him before.

"So… you stalked me?" I asked hesitantly.

"Yes."

"Why?" I couldn't wrap my head around that part. The rest I could at least partially understand.

"I don't know. I couldn't stop myself from doing it. I made sure you got to your car safely after work and into your house after that. Sometimes I would come by in the middle of the night to make sure you were okay and nothing was happening to you. I never wanted to harm you. It was like I couldn't rest or focus on anything else until I knew you were okay. It sounds insane and I'm sure you think I am, but I can't explain it. Once you moved in with me, it all stopped. Hell, once we started seeing each other regularly, the urges lessened greatly for the most part. I knew I would have to tell you one day, I just kept putting it off because I knew it'd freak you out. Any person in their right mind would be upset about someone following them around." He hung his head and shook it slowly.

I stared at him. While I knew I should be upset, I couldn't seem to find the emotions within me. If anything, I felt relieved. He'd never done anything to hurt me, not that I didn't want anyway. He was never malicious or even overly angry with anyone, let alone me. I can only imagine how upsetting and strange it was for a man with so much self-control to feel out of control of his own body and thoughts.

Scooting closer to him, I wrapped my arms around his shoulders and he jumped as if expecting a blow instead of a hug.

"I understand. It's okay. I wish you would've told me earlier and that I wouldn't have had to stumble over it myself, but I do get it. I masturbated in all sorts of places and inappropriate times because of my crazy urges. They weren't things I wanted to do, but I did them anyway because I was compelled to do them. However, if the urges are gone now that I'm here, then things are better. Have you ever done such things to another person?" I asked as the question popped into my head.

"No!" he stated adamantly. "Never. It's always only been you. Something about you, Precious. Something I can't shake."

"Well, good, 'cause if that is the worst you have, then you can't shake me. Almost everything can be talked through as long as you start the conversation. It's secrets that kill," I said before placing a kiss on his temple.

His body vibrated in my arms before he pulled me into his lap, burying his face in my neck.

"What did I do to deserve you? I love you more than life itself," John whispered into my hair.

Chapter Ten

~John~

When Friday rolled around, I could barely contain my excitement. I'd told all my friends that I was no longer going to be helping any of them cover any time on the online site. It was a long time coming, but I hated saying no to people who'd helped me out in the past. Since Alix had found out everything, I wanted nothing more than to spend every moment I could with her. I felt lighter than I had in a long time. It'd been hell hiding something from her. She'd taken the news better than I'd expected — well, once I'd calmed her down.

I'd planned everything for our evening out and hopefully it would all go down as expected. April had left most of my afternoon unscheduled as I'd asked her to so that I could make a few last-minute stops.

After I'd seen my last patient, I'd run across town to the dry cleaners to pick up my favorite suit, then picked up the last couple of items before going home. There wasn't much time before Alix was expected back from her first day of volunteering at the shelter.

In fact, I'd just finished straightening my jacket in the mirror when I heard the front door close, signaling she'd arrived home.

"Babe?" she called out, followed by the clinking of keys as she set them down on the table.

I smiled, knowing her habits.

"In here," I shouted back and waited for her to make it to our room.

She stepped in and stopped to look me over from head to toe, then once more before a smile curled over her lips.

"Wow. You look damn good," she said, licking her bottom lip and walking closer. She tugged on my lapels and went on tiptoe to kiss me firmly. "Are you sure we have to go out tonight? I'd really rather stay here and strip that exquisite suit off you one piece at a time."

"Yes. Although if you are still interested, you can do it when we get back." I winked at her. "I did get you a new dress to wear."

"You did? What's the big occasion?" She wiggled her eyebrows before turning to stalk into the closet in search of the new item. After a moment, she came back out with a frown. "I don't see it."

"That's because it's on the bed." I nodded toward it and her cheeks turned pink.

Picking up the small, bright blue dress, she held it up then pressed it to her front.

"Short and sassy. Good thing I have you to keep any stray hands from getting too close." She giggled, then set it down and started stripping.

I was happy to see the boring tan pants and polo shirt go. Slinky, sexy and soft looked so much better on her.

When she moved to the dresser to take out a garter belt, stockings and a matching set of panties and bra, I felt my dick thicken and lengthen. She knew exactly what buttons to push to get me hard.

Smiling, she walked past me into the bathroom in her comfortable underwear. After a quick rinse in the shower, she jumped out and strolled past me completely nude with water droplets still sticking in various places where she'd missed them.

"Precious," I growled in warning. It was taking all my control to keep my hands off her when she taunted me like she was. However, knowing all the plans I'd put into place, I refused to give in.

Slowly, she pulled on one stocking, connected it to the garter belt then did the same to the other one. She put on her panties and bra next, then finally the dress.

"How's it look?" she asked, walking to the full-length mirror in the corner of the room.

The bottom of the dress barely covered the lacy tops of the stockings and the back dipped low enough it almost revealed her bra strap, but it perfectly accentuated her curves and cleavage.

"Simply divine," I said, walking up behind her and pulling her against me so she could feel just how much I liked it.

"Mmm, good, since you bought it." She grinned at me in the mirror before heading to her jewelry box to retrieve a couple of strands of pearls I'd bought her. Each was a different length and together they drew more attention to her breasts. She fluffed her hair, then turned to look at me. "Ready, sir."

I ushered her to my car, only allowing her to stop to grab her purse. We didn't speak on the drive to the restaurant. Excitement filled the air in the car. The glances we shared said enough words weren't needed. It was a special night, but I wasn't going to tell her why and she knew not to ask. Electricity practically sparked between us as we exited the car.

"Do you have reservations?" the twiggy thing behind the hostess stand asked when we entered the restaurant.

"John O'Roarke," I told her, wrapping my arm around Alix's waist.

We followed the hostess as she led us to our table. While I could tell the girl was trying to catch my attention, I had eyes only for Alix.

"Here we are," the girl said, holding a hand out to emphasize a booth that was in the back of the restaurant, exactly as I'd requested.

I waited until Alix was seated before sliding n across from her. We chatted briefly over what we were going to have before the waiter showed up to take our order, then disappeared again.

"So, what was so special that you set up a date night?" Alix asked, leaning over the table to get closer to me.

"Why does it have to be something special for me to want to take you out for a nice evening?" I asked, lifting an eyebrow.

"You don't have me fooled. There is a reason, I just haven't figured it out yet." She squinted her eyes as if that would help her figure it out.

I laughed and shook my head.

The restaurant was quiet with a romantic ambiance, but it was also the first place Alix and I had gone on a date to. I didn't know if she remembered that or not, but it was why I'd brought her there.

Our food arrived and we ate in relative silence. As we finished, she asked about my day and clients, but seemed to have realized she'd just have to wait until I was ready to reveal my plans.

When they brought the dessert platter to the table to show us all that was offered, there was a ring box in the front.

Alix looked at me wide-eyed and I looked from her to the server with a similar, surprised expression.

"Uh…" I trailed off, looking back to the box and the server before shaking my head. That wasn't supposed to be there!

He cleared his throat and turned a bright shade of red.

"Oh. This isn't for your table. I'm incredibly sorry," he said, snatching the box up and tucking it into his apron.

"I think we are good without dessert. Just the check, please," I said tensely and he scooted away. I took a deep breath and turned toward Alix.

"Well, that was a bit awkward." She laughed, rubbing the back of her neck. Her face was pink with her own embarrassment.

"Yes."

I didn't say anything else and paid when our bill arrived. Then we walked back out to the car. I could tell Alix was disappointed. She'd hoped that ring was for her, but I wasn't going to call her on it, not until we were alone. I prayed that I could save the evening from that little mishap.

Once we were both settled in, I turned to her with one hand on the steering wheel and placed the other one on her thigh.

"Precious, did that ring look like anything I would have given you?" I asked, because really, it wasn't my style or hers at all. She might have been excited for a "real" proposal, but the ring wouldn't have been right for us, nor would asking in such a cheesy way.

"No. I still would've said yes," she said, slumping in her seat.

I forced her to look at me by pressing a finger to her cheek. When her eyes met mine, I closed the distance between us to place a soft kiss on her lips.

"You already said yes, Precious," I reminded her, threading my fingers into her hair.

"I know. Never mind. It's nothing," she said, waving a hand through the air and forcibly straightening her back and shoulders.

I watched her for a moment before taking back my hand. I sighed softly before starting the car and heading to our next destination. The excitement from before was gone, but I kept silent until I pulled into the parking lot across from The Scene.

"Oh. I didn't know we were coming here," she said, looking at me with a whole different type of thrill in her eyes than earlier in the evening.

"Mmm, yes." I smiled and exited the car. It had been awhile since we'd been to the club, one of the first places we'd met and gotten intimate.

After helping her from the car, I wrapped a hand around the back of her neck. It was a show of dominance and she melted against me with a soft moan.

Inside, she handed over her purse to the woman waiting behind the desk, then without any other interruptions, we went to my room. I shed my jacket and draped it over a chair in the corner while she watched me.

"Strip," I said while undoing the buttons on my shirt.

She shimmied out of the dress. The wiggle of her body drew my attention and made me pause. A small smile pulled at her lips when she caught the hesitation in my movements, then she sank to her knees on the padded section of the floor, bowing her head.

I quickly finished removing my shirt and tossed it aside, then walked around my submissive. So perfect. So mine.

Once I completed a circle, I stopped in front of her with my feet shoulder-width apart. My cock was already getting excited just seeing her half nude and handing over her control to me.

"Stand," I demanded.

She gracefully did as instructed, keeping her head down.

Moving close to her, my hands glided from her shoulders to her hands, then I threaded my fingers with hers. I forced her to lift her arms over her head as I pressed my body against hers. The feel of the silk bra against my bare chest made desire throb through me and a soft sound escaped from Alix's lips.

I released her and trailed the tips of my fingers down the sensitive underside of her arms and sides. Stepping around her, I grabbed a length of rope from the nearby table. It only took a few movements before her wrists were securely bound together, then I slipped the knot over a hook hanging from the ceiling.

"Now you can't go anywhere," I murmured against her neck before licking a line up to her ear. Dragging a hand around her hip, I stepped back in front of her. I reached up and removed all of her necklaces. "Wouldn't want these to get dirty."

She bit her bottom lip, holding back a protest.

I've never taken my pearls off her before so I knew she wanted to ask why I was doing it that time, but she didn't.

Once more, I stepped close to her and kissed a line down her throat, between her breasts and then down her stomach before lowering myself to my knees to continue downward. At the top of her panties, I kissed from hip to hip. Nuzzling my face into her silk-covered mound, I slid my palms up her legs until I could hook a finger under the elastic keeping the material on. Yanking downward, I took them off.

She lifted one foot then the other so I could completely remove them.

I reached between her thighs to grip an ass cheek in each hand, bringing her to my mouth so I could tease her pussy.

My tongue traced all along her slit, tasting her arousal while my lungs filled with her unique scent. That combination along with the sight I was greeted with when I looked upward had my dick throbbing and begging to be released.

The more I tasted her, the more I thought I could stay there forever, with her on my face and filling all my senses.

"Oh, sir! Please let me come. I want to come on your face," Alix begged from above me.

Pushing two fingers into her so I could nail her sweet spot, I lifted my head enough to answer her.

"Come for me, Precious. Let me hear how good I make you feel. Show me how much you want my cock in you," I said, looking up the line of her body to where her breasts were heaving from her rapid breaths, then farther to where her head was thrown back in pleasure, her bound wrists coming into view occasionally as she writhed on me. Lowering my face back to suck her clit into my mouth, I moved my fingers faster in and out of her.

"Yes... Oh, yes... Master..." Alix barely breathed the words between gasping for air. Her thighs tensed around me seconds before her pussy clamped down on my fingers and she sharply arched against her restraints as her orgasm flashed through her.

I lapped at her, capturing all of her release before standing again. Quickly, I undid my pants and shucked the rest of my clothing. I couldn't resist stroking myself while watching her come back down from the high of getting off. Precome leaked out to help lubricate the glide of skin on skin.

Alix blinked her eyes open after a moment and immediately her eyes locked on my cock. She bit down on her bottom lip as a shiver went through her.

"Want a taste?" I asked her and she nodded right away. I smiled and released my hard length before walking over to the prepared table and picking up a knife. I locked eyes with her for a moment to make sure she was okay, then slipped the blade under a bra strap. Once it broke free, I did the same to the other side, then between the cups, and it fell to the ground around her feet. Without being asked or directed to do so, Alix kicked it away, knowing I wouldn't want it in the way.

I couldn't help the spark of pride that rushed up my spine; she knew me so well. After placing the knife back where I got it, I stepped behind her and wrapped my arms around her, taking her breasts in my hands.

"You are so fucking perfect," I said against her skin while thrusting my hips against her ass. My cock slid between her pert, round cheeks.

"Thank you, sir," she replied, tilting her head to give me more access to her neck.

Sighing, I let go of her and picked up a spoon sitting in a crockpot filled with melted chocolate that I'd arranged to have waiting for us.

I pressed the back of the spoon to her nipple and she gasped at the heat, then I took it away leaving behind a thick smudge of chocolate. Grabbing another spoon, I replaced the first one and traced the outer edge of her clean, puckered nipple before smashing the chocolate-filled side against it.

"It's so hot, sir," Alix gasped, but held still.

The chocolate would cool quickly, giving an intense change in temperature on her nipples, which was exactly why I liked using the hot spoons to apply it.

"Do you want me to stop?" I asked even as I traded spoons again. Before she could answer I drizzled chocolate over her neck and lips, then licked and sucked along the path I'd made.

"No, sir," she said, shaking her head.

"Good." I smiled against her lips. "Turns out I want dessert after all."

She simply moaned because I dropped my head to suck her nipple into my mouth and flicked my tongue repeatedly over it, making sure it was clean.

I did the same to the other coated peak, then reached up to unhook her wrists.

Alix dropped her wrists in front of her as a pained groan slipped from her parted lips.

"Knees," I told her, ignoring the sound.

While she lowered herself, I took a moment to cover my dick with the thick substance, then stood in front of her. I nudged her lips with my coated tip and she sucked me in.

"Oh…" She managed to moan the word around my length as she took more of me into her mouth.

It didn't take her long to have a smooth, bobbing rhythm as she practically inhaled every inch of me.

I let her continue as long as I could until I had to stop or come.

"Stop. Get on the bed," I told her as I stepped back, forcing her to stop whether she wanted to listen or not.

"Yes, sir," Alix said and quickly climbed onto the bed.

I unplugged the little pot of chocolate and moved it to the bedside so it was closer. Picking up one of the spoons, I knelt on the bed next to her. I drew patterns all over her abdomen before moving to include her breasts in the action. Finally, I dipped lower and let a whole spoonful run down between her spread thighs.

It was time to satisfy my sweet tooth; I smiled to myself and went to town cleaning off the most sexy body I'd ever seen. The more I licked the more she moaned and wiggled under me. Until I got to her pussy. As soon as my mouth was on her, she got much louder and was on the edge of coming almost immediately.

"Oh, sir, please. Let me come. It hurts, I need it so bad," she whined.

"Not yet, Precious," I said, shaking my head between her thighs, which only made her cry out again and an evil smile tug at my lips.

Once I thought she was clean enough, I knelt between her thighs and lined my cock up before thrusting into her in one swift motion. I lowered myself down onto my elbow so we were inches apart as I held completely still while filling her.

"Precious?" I asked and waited until her eyes met mine, all the haze of lust fading away slowly when she saw I was serious. "Will you wear my collar? Will you forever be my submissive while letting me take care of you as your dom? Let me give you everything you need in the bedroom and outside. Wear a sign of my ownership of you. Commit yourself only to me for the foreseeable future."

"Absolutely, sir." Alix didn't even hesitate in her answer.

I had the collar under the pillow, but it'd have to wait to be put on because the only thing I could think of was keeping my dick as deep inside her as I could until I spilled my seed there and forced her to keep it inside her.

My hips automatically snapped forward when I tried to withdraw from her and both of us groaned out. Alix's bound hands came down to wrap around my neck and pull me into a kiss before moving back over her head.

We kept kissing, passionate, deep, wet until she came around me, moaning into my mouth as she did so. Then even though we were both struggling to breathe, she kept kissing me so I kept kissing her until I couldn't control my body anymore and my release exploded from within and I tore my lips from her to grunt loudly. With each spurt of come, I bucked against her harder than the time before, shoving her up the bed as I did so.

When I finally stopped spewing and collapsed on my side next to her, I had to close my eyes because I was dizzy.

The back of her hand ran down my cheek and I opened my eyes again.

"I love you," she whispered.

"I love you too," I whispered back as I reached under my pillow to retrieve the collar I'd meant to give her earlier. I sat up and helped Alix up as well. Pushing her hair over her shoulders, I wrapped the thick silver band around her neck and fastened it in the back. There was a large pearl that dangled from the front and one from the chain in the back. A tiny lock kept the collar from being taken off without my consent.

"It's beautiful," Alix said, her voice breaking.

"Nothing less for the most precious person in the world," I told her as I slowly unwrapped her wrists. "Let's go home. I have one more surprise for you?"

"Another surprise? I don't think anything gets better than this," she said, running her hand over the band around her neck.

"I didn't say it was better, just that it was another one." I smiled and started redressing.

Once we were both as presentable as we were going to get, we drove back to our house.

"I love my collar, sir," Alix said, breaking the silence in the car just as we pulled into the drive.

"I'm glad." I looked at her in the dark space. "Are you ready for the final surprise?"

"I don't know. After the last one I'm sticky, smell like dessert and still worn out from the amazing orgasms you gave me, but I think I can stand a bit more." She smiled as she fingered the pearl hanging from the choker. "For you I can do anything."

"We shall see," I said before climbing from the car, then helping her out. My palm rested against her lower back as I led her to the front door. I held out the keys for her. "Here, you open it."

She gave me an odd look but took the keys from my hand. It took her a moment to find the right key to open the door, then push it open as if expecting something to happen.

Nothing did.

Chapter Eleven

~Alix~

It had been an interesting night. After the romantic dinner followed by someone else's engagement ring on the dessert tray, I was upset. Yes, John had proposed, but I still didn't have a ring and he'd stopped offering to take me to look so I was wondering if he'd changed his mind. Then he'd mentioned that the ring was completely wrong for us and I had to agree.

We hadn't been to The Scene in a long time since most of what we needed was at the house and we didn't play in public often; however, there was something incredibly sexy about being there that only added to our time together.

I still couldn't believe he'd given me an actual collar and claimed me as his own forever in the BDSM world. It was beautiful from what I'd seen of it, and I could feel the large pearl hanging down from the front which completely fit us.

Sadly, even though I'd completely enjoyed the evening, I was ready for a shower and bed. I highly doubted after everything I'd be getting the ring I so craved anytime soon. Not from the way his face had paled at dinner.

There was one surprise left, though and I tried to keep my energy and smile for him instead of feeling let down. It's funny how I hadn't even expected him to propose or get a ring, but it was like now that he'd asked and said he'd do it right I couldn't get it out of my head.

When I opened the door, I expected there to be something right there as the final surprise, but the living room looked exactly as we'd left it. I frowned; I couldn't help it. Why did he have me open the door if it wasn't right there?

I set the keys on the side table with my purse and started a path to the bedroom. John was following after, adding his wallet to the other items.

"Am I supposed to be looking somewhere special for this surprise?" I asked as I went. My feet were starting to hurt from my tall heels and I wanted to get out of them before I went on this scavenger hunt or whatever would lead me to the last thing.

"Nope," John said, making me jump. He was right behind me. His warm breath glided over my bare shoulder as his arms wrapped around my waist. "You okay, Precious? You seem tense all of a sudden."

"Yeah, I'm just tired. You worked me hard tonight," I admitted. At least that part was true.

"Well, then let's get you into the shower. We can forget about the rest of what I had planned." He ran the stubble on his jaw over my shoulder until his nose nudged my neck and I tilted my head to the opposite side.

"I'll just feel bad, since you planned everything and now I'm ruining it." I frowned but closed my eyes, leaning back against his hard body.

"It'll hold. Let's get you undressed." He slid his hands down from my waist to the hem of the dress to dip his hands under it. His hands moved upward until he found my garter belt, which he unsnapped, then he worked on undoing the clasps which held up my stockings. I hadn't put my panties back on when we'd left The Scene because I couldn't find where they'd been thrown.

John knelt behind me and helped roll down each stocking then removed them and my heels along with the garter belt before standing once more.

"Let me turn off the light before we go to the bathroom," he said, leaving me in the middle of the room.

When he flipped off the light, I gasped. In bright green letters that were stuck on the wall behind our bed was "Will You Marry Me?" I spun around where John had turned off the light to find him right behind me on one knee with a ring box in his hand.

"So, will you marry me? Will you be my wife? Not just my submissive, but the woman who makes me laugh, who challenges me in every aspect of life, the woman who makes me happier than any man has the right to be. Let me cherish you and give you all that I am. Say that you'll spend the rest of your life with me and allow me to spend the rest of mine with you," John said. The hand holding the box trembled.

"Yes. Like I could ever be happy with anyone else," I said as tears ran down my face. This was the proposal I'd been waiting for and the platinum ring was absolutely perfect. A pearl sat in the middle of the ring with a silver band diagonally across it and small diamonds on either side.

John slid the ring onto my finger and stood to pull me into his arms.

"How was that?" he asked with a shaky smile.

"I couldn't have dreamed of a better proposal," I said before kissing him, sliding my tongue into his mouth and grinding my body against his to show him just how wonderful it was and how turned on it made me to see this soft, unsure side of the man who was always so secure in all that he did.

"Make love to me, John," I breathed against his lips.

His hands grabbed my thighs and he hiked me up until I had no other option but to wrap my legs around his waist.

I laughed as he walked us to the bed and tenderly laid me down before climbing between my thighs.

After long, passionate kisses, John finally shed his pants and made slow, sweet love to me until both of us passed out from exhaustion.

The next couple of weeks passed in a blur as I got used to volunteering at the shelter. Initially I'd only planned to spend a day or two a week there, but once I found out how short-staffed and funded they were, I ended up spending a few hours a day there. While I never worked with Mariah, I usually passed her on my way in or out.

She was always friendly and would stop to chat for a minute or two, but then would excuse herself without once giving me a creepy vibe or making any signs that made me doubt her path to recovery.

One day she stopped me as I was coming in and looked around to make sure there wasn't anyone else there.

"So, I've been wondering if maybe you would be interested in joining me for a coffee or something. You know, put all this craziness behind us. I'd really like to get to know you better," she said.

I tried not to grimace. While I knew she was trying to be nice, I just didn't know that I was ready to be meeting her when it was just us.

"Look, you can bring a friend or something if that makes you feel better," she said with a hopeful smile on her face.

"I'll have to see when my friend is available and let you know," I told her and was saved from having to say anything else because my phone started ringing. Looking at the screen, I smiled. "Speak of the devil. I'll catch you later."

"Okay. Let me know," she said, then with a small wave she walked away.

While I watched her go, the phone rang again and I answered it.

"Jennifer?" I asked.

"Hi! What are you up to? Want to go out today? I'm *so* bored," she replied in her high-energy tone of voice.

"Sure. I need to go home, shower and change first but I could use some girl time." I knew John would be busy with work and I hadn't seen her in quite a while.

She told me she'd be by in an hour to get me so I hurried home to get ready. When she rang the bell, I was waiting in a pair of jeans and a tank top with my hair pulled back in a ponytail.

"Oh, look at you looking all housewife-ish," she said, laughing when I opened the door to find her wearing a short pair of shorts and a tight top.

"Well… That's pretty much what I am now." I shrugged.

"Wait. WHAT. IS. THAT?" Jennifer screeched in a high-pitched squeal as she grabbed my left hand to examine my engagement ring. "You didn't tell me!"

"Oh, uh, yeah. Sorry about that." I smiled shyly. It hadn't really occurred to me to call anyone to tell them about it. Not like we were planning on having an engagement party or even the wedding yet. As far as I knew, the wedding wasn't even going to be an event, just a courtroom with the two of us and whatever witnesses we needed. Neither of us had family we wanted there and not many friends either. We weren't getting married for any of them, anyway — it was for us and us alone.

"And is that a *collar*? What is going *on* with you? I feel like you leave out all the good stuff when you talk to me," she said, exasperated, as she flicked the pearl hanging from my choker.

"Don't be ridiculous," I sighed. "It all just happened a little while ago. I didn't realize it was such a big deal."

I didn't, either. I wasn't a girly girl and didn't really share private details of my life with anyone. While I talked with Jennifer every few days it was usually her talking while I listened since I didn't have much to share or would talk about my time volunteering.

"Well, it is a big deal. A *huge* deal. I forgive you though. But I can't say I'm not a bit jealous because, damn, girl, your man is fine and the female population will be weeping the day he is completely off the market." She smiled even as I grabbed my stuff and walked out of the house with her on my heels.

"I hate to be the one to tell you, but he's completely off the market now," I admitted.

"Sure. I know that, but there are some out there that think he's still an option until he is married and it's legal."

I shook my head as we both climbed into her car. Some women were just crazy and that's all there was to it.

We spent the next couple of hours shopping, or more like Jennifer shopped and I kept her company. Since I didn't have a job I wasn't spending what little money I had saved. I did pick up a couple new bras and matching panties since John liked to destroy them on a fairly regular basis, but I charged that to the credit card he'd gotten in my name.

By the time Jennifer dropped me back at the house, I was exhausted and had remembered why I could only take her in small doses. She was a blast to be around, but she had so much more energy than I did.

"Those are some sexy panties you bought," she had said on the drive back. "I was going to suggest you pick up something naughty to surprise John with, but if that's what you're wearing on a regular basis..."

I laughed as she trailed off.

"What can I say, he inspires me to wear the sexiest panties I can find. Not like it matters. I could wear nothing or granny panties and he'd still have a hard time keeping his hands off me. That's just how he is," I sighed wistfully while shaking my head.

"Damn! As if I wasn't already jealous of you," Jennifer said, wiping a fake tear from her cheek. "I swear the man is too perfect."

"Oh, no. He's not perfect. There are definitely things that require work and understanding in order to make our relationship work, but that's how every relationship is, right?" I said with a shrug. I wasn't going to disclose either of our issues as it was none of her business.

She didn't say anything after that and I knew I'd won the discussion. John might be the most exquisite man in the world, but he wasn't without faults and no relationship was without its hiccups and bumps.

I had asked her about going out with me and Mariah for coffee while we'd been shopping and as expected, she'd agreed to be there for me. She was curious to set her eyes on John's ex more than anything.

A week later, all three of us met at a small café late in the morning. I hadn't told John where I was going and with whom, or rather I'd left out the part where Mariah would be there and was the main reason behind the gathering. For some reason, I still hadn't told him that Mariah was at the shelter, either. I suppose it was because she'd seemed as normal as any other person and I didn't want him to make me stop volunteering simply due to her being there.

Jennifer and I were seated by a window in the shop when Mariah joined us. Of course she looked like the perfect specimen of beauty that I'd come to expect from her. Her long blonde hair flowed around her in waves and seemed to blow in a non-existent breeze. Her jeans showed off her narrow hips and slim thighs while her top emphasized her perky, full breasts and flat stomach.

"There's Mariah," I said, pointing her out with a small wave when I caught her eye.

Jennifer scoffed under her breath and it made me smile to know I wasn't the only one irritated by her perfection.

"John dated that woman? They'd make pretty babies, that's for sure," Jennifer said in a hushed voice.

"Uh…" I frowned and flashed her a look that made sure she knew that wasn't the correct response.

"It's too bad for her that he's over his head in love with you," she quickly added.

I held in a laugh as Mariah sat across the table from us.

"Good morning ladies," Mariah said, flipping her hair over one shoulder. Her smile seemed genuine as she held a hand out to Jennifer. "I'm Mariah."

"Jennifer," my friend responded, extending her own hand.

"I'm so happy we could all get together," Mariah said as the waiter stopped by to take her order. She ordered something that made my teeth hurt from how sweet it sounded. Once the waiter moved on, she turned her attention back to us. "This year has been so… interesting. I'm just glad I didn't hurt anyone before I got help."

"Yes, that's a good thing," Jennifer spoke up before I could. "Not that you didn't try."

Mariah lowered her head and nodded slowly.

"Yes, I did. I've already apologized to Alix, but I know I still owe Alix and John for forcing me to see what I was doing was wrong. And I really, truly feel sorry for the way I behaved. It's so embarrassing when I think about it," Mariah admitted as she picked at the napkin on the table. "However, that's not why I wanted to meet today. Well, sort of. I wanted to show you that I'm not the same person and I want to be friends."

She'd already said as much to me before, but I suspected she wanted Jennifer to know as well as reinforce it all to me again.

After her coffee was delivered, we managed to get over the awkward, stilted way things started. It was mostly because Jennifer refused to allow any conversation to remain boring for any length of time. She had both of us laughing and talking like old friends before long.

I still didn't share much about my life with John, but it wasn't anything different from how I was with Jennifer. John was a private topic and I didn't like giving away anything about our relationship if I didn't have to.

By the time we parted ways a few hours later, we'd all come to the agreement we'd meet again in a few days for another coffee date because it had gone so well.

Over the next two weeks, we all met up a couple of times, each one becoming more and more comfortable. I really felt like Mariah had changed her ways and she was actually kind of funny and sweet. She often talked about her boyfriend, Bry, and their relationship woes and triumphs. Sometimes I wondered if she was hoping I'd share the same stuff about John's and my relationship, but she never seemed disappointed when I didn't. I'd caught her eyeing my ring a few times, but I couldn't blame her for that as it was beautiful and hard not to be impressed by.

One day when it was just Jennifer and I, she turned and looked at me with the most serious expression I'd ever seen on her face before.

"Uh oh. I don't like that look," I told her, but she smiled.

"You need to have an engagement party," she said, grabbing my left hand and squeezing.

"Why?" I asked, curiously.

"Because! You need to announce to everyone that you are getting married and show off that beautiful man of yours. I'll even throw it for you and do all the work of putting it together if you don't want to do it."

"No. That's not it. I just don't know who we would even invite. I mean, it's not like we have a ton of people to really tell. Plus, most of them already know," I said, shrugging. I really didn't want her to get the idea of inviting my estranged family, not that she knew about them, but that didn't mean she couldn't find out if she dug. Oh, how I hated the internet sometimes. Somethings were meant to be left in the past. A shiver ran up my spine at the thought of seeing any of them again.

"Girl, it's not just about making the announcement. It's showing that you are happy to be joining your lives together. Let the people from both of your lives mingle and get to know each other, as from now on it's likely that they'll be seeing each other at any event you go to or throw as a couple. Then there's the whole gift aspect. Free stuff! That's an excellent reason alone. Plus, who doesn't love a good party?" She was practically bouncing in her seat as she excitedly listed off the reasons. "And let's just admit it, you and John likely aren't going to have a big wedding because neither of you are like that, so this will be the one chance for everyone to get together and celebrate. Come on. *Please.*"

She was begging, the look on her face said I might as well kick her non-existent dog as turn her down.

Sighing, I said, "Sure. Fine. We'll have a party. *But* I have to make sure John is okay with it before we start planning anything."

Jennifer squealed and hugged me just as Mariah sat down at the table. I prayed she'd not find out the single secret I kept from every single person in my life. If my family showed up, the party would instantly be ruined.

"Wow, what did I miss?" Mariah asked, smiling even as her eyes bounced from one of us to the other.

"We are throwing an engagement party!" Jennifer literally bounced in her seat.

"Oh, how exciting," Mariah gasped, holding a hand up to her chest. A sad look crossed her face a moment later. "I hope it's beautiful."

"If, and that's a big if, John says the party is okay, you'll get an invite too," I said, and her face brightened again.

"That's very sweet of you; however, I doubt John would be okay with me coming so don't feel obligated to include me. I'll just hear all about it afterwards. It's okay," she said, but I could tell she wanted to be included even if she was trying to be nice about it.

"I'll talk to him about it, okay?" I tried to reassure her. I considered her one of my friends and didn't want her feeling left out. Not to mention, we might need the extra pair of hands to get everything ready.

The rest of our coffee date reverted to the easy conversation that had become our way, leaving parties and engagements behind.

***

That night when John got home from work, I had dinner ready and put it on the table once he'd changed. I let him tell me about his day while we ate. Once we'd done the dishes and were cuddling on the couch, I decided to broach the topic.

"So, I saw Jennifer for coffee this morning," I started, pulling back to look at his face.

"Yes, you told me that you had planned to do so," he said.

"Well, an interesting topic came up and I wanted to talk to you about it," I said, taking a deep breath.

He lifted one eyebrow but stayed silent.

"She wants us to throw an engagement party," I revealed, not sure why my stomach was a bundle of knots. John didn't know about my past, not that part anyway and I wanted it to stay that way. I didn't want to drag all the horrid memories out from where I'd locked them away.

"That sounds like an excellent idea. Then I can show off my beautiful fiancée," he said with a wicked smile on his face.

I loved that smile and I couldn't help but smile back.

"There is one other thing…" I trailed off and couldn't help but tense before I finally told him the truth. "I'd like to invite Mariah to the party."

He sucked in a sharp breath and I felt him stiffen next to me.

"Why?" he finally asked.

"Well, I've run into her a few times and we've been talking. I think she's gotten help and is not the crazy woman who tried to break us up. She's really different now," I said, talking quickly.

"Wait. Say that again. You've run into her and haven't told me?" John interrupted and I could tell from his tone that he wasn't happy with me.

"She's always been really nice and sweet. I mean, she's apologized more times than I can count about how she behaved. She even has a boyfriend she's been seeing for six months now. I just think this would be a good way to show that there are no hurt feelings." I tried to ignore his question and hoped if I explained enough he would let it go.

"Oh, so not only did you not tell me you had seen her, but you want me to forgive her for trying to take you away from me?" John pushed off the couch as tension radiated off him. When I started speaking again, he glared at me angrily. "Tell me how long this has been going on? How long have you been hiding this from me?"

I cleared my throat and looked down at my lap.

"A few months," I said, barely audible. "Well, sort of."

"Clarify. Now." John put his hands on his hips angrily.

"Well, I ran into her a while ago and she's the one who recommended I volunteer at the shelter. I saw her a few times in passing there. Well, I saw her almost every day really, but she was always really sweet. One day she asked me to meet her for coffee…"

"You. Met. Her. For. Coffee?" He paused for emphasis on each word as if he truly couldn't believe what I was saying.

"I took Jennifer with me. There were always other people around in case she went crazy, but she didn't. She hasn't. I swear I did everything I could to stay safe," I said, once again meeting his gaze.

"Yet you didn't tell me." He looked disappointed in me.

"I didn't want to upset you, but I couldn't help wanting to get to know her. She might've been crazy but she *is* your past, and she's not as bad as I thought she was. I can see why you dated her," I admitted.

"She was crazy as hell when I dated her, so I don't know how she can be all that different now, no matter what you say." John shook his head before running a hand through his hair.

"She said she got help. That she knew she had to after the last time she tried to come between us," I told him, standing and resting my hands on his shoulders. "I think it would be good for both of us to know that she won't be coming between us in the future, that she is in the past and will be staying there and out of our relationship."

"Precious, I don't think it's a good idea. I'd rather just not see her and not have you talking to her," he said, wrapping an arm around my waist. "I'm not happy that you hid that you were meeting with her from me, but I understand why because I would have told you not to. However, if I find out you are hiding something like this again, I will beat your ass until you can't sit down for a week."

"But, sir, I think both of us would like it way too much for it to be considered a punishment," I whispered seductively as I wrapped my arms around his neck. My fingers slid into the hair at his nape. "However, maybe you should do it now to remind me why I should tell you everything."

"Oh, you need a reminder? I think that could be arranged." He yanked me against his body by my hips before he tugged my head back by my ponytail. John nipped my neck with his teeth before spinning me around and bending me over the couch.

My cheek rested on the back cushion as he flipped my dress up over my hips, revealing that I wasn't wearing any panties.

"Mmm, Precious. You little tease. I think that earns you a few extra spankings," John said while his hands rubbed my ass cheeks, warming my flesh.

He slapped each side a few times lightly; not hard enough to hurt, but they brought blood to the surface in order to prep me for a much harder spanking.

I gripped the couch on either side of where my head rested in anticipation of the strength of the incoming blows. It was a good thing I did too because the first couple of times his palm landed on my cheeks I wanted to cry out, but managed to refrain from doing so. I was panting shallowly and trying to breathe through the pain when he kicked my feet farther apart.

"Now comes the reminder you asked for," John purred, running a palm down my spine, over my burning bottom to slip between my thighs. His fingers teased over my damp flesh briefly before his hand descended upon my rear once more.

Even though tears filled my eyes and I wanted the spanking to end, I couldn't help but be turned on by it as well. When John's hands were on me, his dominant side in charge, I loved it. He always managed to turn pain into an erotic, sensual experience. Each time his palm met my fevered skin, my pussy contracted and I got wetter and needier.

I'd lost track of how many spankings I'd received, but it didn't matter; somewhere in the middle I stopped counting and started moaning instead. While my skin was raw and felt like it was on fire, I prayed that John would follow up the next spanking with a rough and hard thrust of his dick inside me.

There was nothing that compared to getting a brutal fucking after a good spanking. Ass painfully tender, hips grinding into it, making it flare to life as he filled me, stretching me with his beautiful, thick cock.

Absolutely nothing in the world could touch us when we got to this place. It wasn't just me who was on a wild ride, but John too. As high as I climbed, he was right there with me and that only made me go higher.

Finally the slaps stopped; the only sounds in the room were our breathing. I thought he was finished, then the sound of metal grinding against metal as he undid his zipper came and my breathing sped up even more. Not a moment later, he was balls-deep in me.

I cried out and arched my back from the sudden intrusion.

"Yeah, squeeze my dick nice and tight," John moaned as he paused for a moment. His fingers gripped my hips tightly as he started moving. Long, slow withdrawal. Fast and hard thrust in.

Each time he filled me, he swiveled his hips, rubbing them across my sore behind.

"Sir!" I cried out from the sweet pleasure combined with the burning addition of the skin-on-skin friction.

"That's right, Precious. Say my name. Tell me who owns you, who possesses you," John grunted the words as he slammed into me over and over, vigorously filling me only to slowly retreat time and time again.

"Sir... Master... John..." I gasped between each word. My fingers crushed the cushion as savage, searing warmth filled me.

John grabbed a fistful of my hair and pulled my head back so he could kiss and nip my throat as he continued to fuck me. His other hand slipped around my hip to vigorously rub my swollen clit.

"S... sir, I'm going to come," I panted.

"Come all over my cock," he hoarsely demanded, slapping hard at my clit with his palm while his hips thumped against my sore ass.

I choked on a wail as every part of me pulsed and heat seared through my veins.

"Yes… Yes… YES," John whispered each word until he yanked back harder on my hair and his fingers dug into the flesh of my thigh as he too found his release.

My hair slid through his fingers as he relaxed over my back and both of us fought to breathe while staying on our feet.

"How was that for a reminder of why you talk to me?" John breathed against my neck after a moment.

"It couldn't have been better," I sighed and smiled.

Chapter Twelve

~John~

I was sitting in my office at work between patients when my phone rang unexpectedly. I'd texted Alix only an hour before to let her know this was my last client of the day and she'd said she was already home getting dinner ready, so I knew it wasn't her.

"Hello," I answered, wondering who it was that April had put them through to me.

"You need to come home now."

Okay, so maybe it *would* be Alix, since that was who was on the other end of the phone.

"Why? What's going on?" I asked.

She didn't sound upset or mad, so I was curious since she rarely made demands that required me to leave work. Even when she'd been working, she'd never demanded I come to her, but requested or told me not to and I would go to her anyway because I knew she needed me.

"John. Come. Home. Now."

She was pissed. That was clear from her tone of voice that time.

"All right. Let me see if we can cancel this client and I'll be there as soon as I can," I told her before hanging up.

April was sitting at her desk as I expected. She was inputting invoices and turned to look at me.

"What's up?" she asked.

"I need to go. Can you cancel my final appointment?" I sighed. I wasn't looking forward to going home to an angry Alix.

"Sure. I need to talk to you first though," she said. She fidgeted nervously.

"Can it wait until tomorrow?"

"I've already put it off too long," she said, shaking her head. "Look, I'm pregnant. I have to give you my two-week notice. My boyfriend is moving us to live near his parents so they can help us care for the baby. I hate to leave so soon, but none of this was planned. I'm sorry."

"Uh... wow. Okay. It'll be fine. I wish you the best though." I tried not to grind my teeth. As if I wasn't stressed enough with this upcoming engagement party with my crazy ex, Alix was upset with me and now I had to find a new secretary. "Please cancel that appointment. I've got to go."

She nodded and I rushed out to my car so I could race home.

Alix greeted me at the door with red-rimmed eyes and my laptop in her arm.

"Precious?" I stepped closer to her, but she stepped away, swiping at her cheek.

"I thought you said you were done with the stalking shit," she angrily snarled at me.

"I am," I said, unsure where she was going with it. She had seemed okay after the night I'd confessed everything to her last week.

"Well, John, then you might want to explain this to me, and talk real fast because I'm about ten seconds from walking out the door and never coming back." Alix stalked to the kitchen and set down the laptop. She opened it, then spun it around for me to see.

"Wha..." I trailed off upon seeing the first picture. It was Alix. Asleep. In our bed. "What the fuck?"

I clicked for the next photo to show up and it was another image of her. And another one. And another. It was clear they were taken on different nights — the bedding changed, as did her outfits, if she was wearing anything at all.

"I didn't take these," I admitted as I continued to flip through the images in shock.

"Really, John? You expect me to believe that? They are on your computer and no one else would be able to take such intimate pictures of me in *our* bed in *our* house." Alix crossed her arms over her chest, anger radiating from her.

"Precious..." I started, but she cut me off.

"Do *not* call me that right now," she spat.

I stepped back from the computer feeling as if she'd slapped me. Not once in all the time we'd been together had she told me I couldn't use the pet name. It stung.

"Alix, I swear on my life that I didn't take these. Not a single one of them. I don't know who took them or how they got on my computer, but it wasn't me. How did you even find them, anyway?" I asked, still trying to figure out what the hell was going on.

"Oh, that's what you want to know? How I found your stash of nude pictures of me?" Alix shook her head and walked away from me.

I knew it was the wrong question, but I was so confused I didn't know what else to say.

"Alix... please," I begged as I followed her.

She slid the strap of her purse over her shoulder and spun to look at me.

"I'm leaving, and until you can answer my questions, the wedding is off. It might still be even if you admit to your problems," she said before escaping out the front door, slamming it in her wake.

I stumbled back to the kitchen and flipped through all the images again and again. Yes, they might have been on my computer, but I had absolutely nothing to do with them. How could I prove that? I looked as guilty as she accused me of being with no way to prove I hadn't done anything.

The same question ran through my head repeatedly until I grabbed a bottle of whiskey and took it to the living room. Skipping a glass, I drank straight out of the bottle until my mind quieted enough for me to think about anything else.

My phone rang and I yanked it out of my pocket, hoping it was Alix. It wasn't.

"Hey Gabe," I said in greeting.

"Man, you sound like shit," Gabe laughed.

"I feel like shit," I confessed.

"I'm coming over," Gabe announced and hung up.

We used to be close, but ever since Alix had come into the picture we'd grown distant. Apparently, he was still determined to be there for me when I needed someone.

A while later, my doorbell rang and I staggered to the door with the bottle of whiskey still in my hand.

"Shit, I'm glad I came over," Gabe said as soon as he saw me. He pushed the door open wider and came in the house.

"Whatever." I shut the door and went back to my wallowing place on the couch.

"Are you going to tell me what's going on or just sit there pickling your liver?" Gabe asked.

I took a deep breath, then another swig out of the bottle, and told Gabe about the pictures.

"So, you really had nothing to do with them?" he questioned again.

"How many fucking times do I have to say that?" I barked at him.

"Okay, okay. So what are you going to do? Who do you think is behind it and why would they do something like that? And why weren't you in the pictures?"

"Fuck if I know. I'm pissed someone was in the house and looking at Alix naked at all, let alone taking pictures of her. What I don't understand is, why put them on my computer? It just doesn't make any damn sense. All I can think of is that whoever is behind it took them after I left for work or something." I leaned my head back on the couch that just last week I'd spanked and fucked Alix on.

"Well..." Gabe sucked in a breath and then shared a plan with me that just might work to get Alix back in my life.

"But that still leaves the motherfucker who did this," I slurred, and took another swig of alcohol.

"Give me the laptop. I'll have my buddy look at it and see what he can find out. He's the best and he'll find out if someone has been fucking around where they shouldn't have been." He held out his hand for the computer.

"It's in the kitchen — and I'll slit your throat if you look at those pictures." I tried to stand, but my legs gave out and I plopped back onto the couch.

Gabe sighed and stood.

"I'll get it. And I'm not going to look at them, don't worry. I can get a free peep show anytime I want."

I groaned and ran a hand over my face before setting the bottle on the table. I needed to be sober if I was going to get Alix back, and now that I had a plan my brain wasn't spinning so wildly, not from the situation at least.

Gabe patted my shoulder from behind.

"Get some sleep and sober up, then get your woman back. I'll be in touch soon," he said before heading for the door.

The next afternoon, I still felt like shit, but I was sober and freshly showered after putting together a plan of action. After making a stop at the hotel, I found that Jennifer had called out for the day and I managed to niggle her address out of the girl who'd taken her shift.

Assuming that was where Alix was, I headed there.

I sat in front of her house for a few minutes before taking a final, fortifying breath and climbing out of my car. I knocked on the door and it was opened by a very angry-looking Jennifer.

"What do you want?" she barked.

"Is Alix here?" I hoped she was, because if she wasn't I didn't know where else to go.

"Why? She doesn't want to see you," she sneered.

"I need to talk to her. Please let me see her. I promise, she'll want to hear what I have to say," I begged the fierce protector filling the doorway.

She sighed and rolled her eyes.

"You stay on the porch. I'm going to see if she is up to listening to your crap," Jennifer said before snapping the door closed in my face.

I stood and waited right where I was. If Alix needed me to show that I wasn't giving up easily or that I'd wait for her, I would do it. I'd do anything she wanted.

Finally the door opened and Alix stepped out in a pair of baggy shorts and an oversized shirt. Her hair was a knotted mess and her eyes were puffy from crying.

"John," she said softly. "What do you want?"

She refused to meet my eyes and I couldn't blame her, but it still burned in my chest. I'd kill for things to go back the way they were just twenty-four hours ago.

"I just came to tell you that I am going to go into a program for in-patient treatment. I have problems and if I need to get help in order to keep you, I will do it happily. Please just give me time before you give up on me." I tried to reach for her hand, but she pulled it away from me. "That is all I came to tell you. I wanted you to hear it from me. I am going to be leaving in two days. You still have a key to our house. Please feel free to use it while I'm gone, or if you are staying here you can get your stuff anytime."

"Okay." She nodded and turned for the door.

"I'm sorry that I have hurt you. I never wanted to hurt you. I only ever wanted to take care of you, to be your world the way you are mine," I admitted quietly, then started down the walkway slowly. While I hadn't taken the pictures, I was willing to take the blame for them if it meant getting my love back. Plus, Gabe had convinced me that not everything I had done involving Alix was okay and it would benefit me to go anyway.

"John?" Alix's voice stopped me.

"Yes?" I turned to look at her and was surprised to have her arms wrap around my waist.

"Thank you," she whispered into my chest.

I kissed the top of her head and folded my arms around her shoulders after the shock passed.

"I want to come home. I want to make this work. Our engagement party is tomorrow and I'd like to still have it. However, I think it'd be a good idea if you went to treatment after it and before our wedding." She lifted her head to look into my eyes as she spoke. "I believe that you didn't want to hurt me and that you love me, but you have to learn what is okay and what isn't if we are going to stay together."

"Absolutely. I want to be better for you," I conceded. My insides were fluttering with excitement at having her in my arms again. She hadn't been gone long, but the fear of never having her there again had been horrifying.

Alix went inside to gather her things and tell Jennifer that she was leaving with me.

I waited outside, afraid of Jennifer tearing into me when Alix and I were still on shaky ground. When she was ready, I took Alix home only for her to tell me that she thought it best if she stayed in the guest room. However, in the middle of the night, she crawled into bed with me and snuggled close.

The next day was a flurry of chaos as Alix and Jennifer got all the last-minute things prepared for the engagement party. It was being held at our house, so I stayed in my office in an attempt to stay away unless they needed my assistance. I'd already taken the day off because I knew I wouldn't be able to focus on my patients' problems, so I didn't have any work to do but I managed to get caught up with little things I normally left for April to handle.

Finally, it was time for me to get ready for the party and I could escape my dungeon for the day. I showered and shaved before walking into the bedroom with a towel wrapped around my hips. Alix was sitting on the edge of the bed waiting for me.

We hadn't spoken a lot since her return and there had definitely not been any sex or touching of any kind, so I was surprised she seemed to want to talk only minutes before people were supposed to start showing up.

Alix had put on a dress that was cinched under her breasts, then flowed out to her knees. Her hair looked beautiful and smooth with a slight curl to it, while her makeup enhanced her natural beauty.

I ached to take her into my arms and muss her hair as I made love to her, but I didn't think that was going to happen so I calmly sat next to her in my towel.

"How are you doing, Alix?" I had yet to use her pet name for fear it'd blow up in my face.

"How are *you* doing?" she repeated the question to me, sidestepping it herself.

"Anxious, I guess," I answered honestly. I wasn't sure how the party was going to go, especially with Alix and I walking on glass when we were supposed to be the happily-engaged couple.

"Me too," she said, looking at me with a shy smile. "Not used to being the center of attention. Not to mention, I'm not entirely sure who-all Jennifer invited."

"It'll be okay. I'll be there by your side the whole time." I clasped her hand in mine.

"I wouldn't expect anything different from you." She squeezed my hand and I felt the pressure around my heart ease with that simple gesture.

She still trusted me.

Chapter Thirteen

~Alix~

I felt overwhelmed and exhausted and the party hadn't even started. It was why I'd sought John out to begin with. I needed him to comfort me and calm the storm brewing inside me. I didn't like the way things were between us. Yes, he needed to get some serious help. Especially after taking pictures of me while I was sleeping. All he had to do was ask and I would've happily let him take whatever pictures he wanted, but the fact he'd done it sneakily and not told me about them crushed me. It was an invasion of what little privacy I had.

I didn't want things to be over between us, not after everything we'd already made it through, but I couldn't allow him to not see the error of his ways. There were just some things you didn't do.

Rising from the bed, I held out my arms and he pulled me close. I breathed in his scent and relaxed in his embrace. Everything would be fine once we got over the newest hurdle. It would. I had to believe it or I'd break down.

After a few long moments, I stepped back and smiled up at John.

"Let's go show everyone what they wish they could have," I said, feeling much better than I had when I'd entered the room.

"Can I get dressed first?" he asked, and I blushed.

"Yes, of course." I'd forgotten he hadn't dressed yet, which showed how stressed I was.

The doorbell rang.

"Why don't you head down and I'll be right there." John kissed my forehead, then released me.

"See you soon," I said and went to get the door.

Jennifer had already greeted Gabe and the two of them were talking quietly. I didn't think they'd met before but it wouldn't be a bad idea for John's good friend to be close to my best friend so I headed to the kitchen instead to double-check everything was ready even though I'd made sure before going to see John. My stomach was a hard ball of nerves, but there'd been no mention of inviting anyone "special" or any surprises so I hoped for the best.

Before long, the house held a dozen people and John had joined the party. When Mariah arrived, the entire room tensed. It was palpable and I started to regret inviting her. Then her boyfriend entered and I stepped back.

It didn't matter that I was in the middle of a conversation. It didn't matter that John was looking at me in concern. Nothing mattered.

I had to get out of the room. Now.

Spinning around, I ran down the hall that led to our bedroom.

John found me hyperventilating in the bathroom with my head between my knees.

"What just happened?" John asked, squatting next to me in his slacks and button-down shirt as he rubbed soothing circles up my back.

"That… That… That was my brother," I managed to get out through my chattering teeth. Violent tremors were running through my body and I couldn't get them to stop.

"I didn't think you had family, or if you did you weren't close to them. Why would he be here?"

I tried to calm down and share the single part of my past that I'd never told him and hadn't spoken about in a very, very long time.

"Come on. Let's go in the bedroom," John said as he clasped my shoulder and tried to pull me to my feet.

I vehemently shook my head and started crying hysterically while repeating, "No."

"Whoa. Calm down," John whispered, scooping me up into his arms. He sat on the cold bathroom floor with me in his lap. "Precious, please talk to me."

I buried my face in his neck and cried.

He held me and rubbed my back until the tears stopped and I was just hiccupping and trembling.

It took me a few tries to wet my tongue enough to speak.

"He raped me." I forced the words out. They were barely audible, but I'd said them. When the world didn't collapse around me, Bryce didn't burst in the door and John didn't react, I swallowed and finished. "He raped me and they didn't believe me."

"Who?" John's voice was tight, like he had a hard time saying the word.

"My parents. They never believed me. No matter how many times he did it. No matter how many times I told them. No one ever believed me. He never stopped. Not until I moved out." The words flowed out now that I'd managed to start. "He beat me, but my parents said it was from being a klutz. Anytime I bled, it was my period being wonky."

I shook my head as all the horrible words my parents called me came back. All the embarrassment I dealt with at school when everyone called me a slut because of the rumors Bryce spread. The memories of him forcing me against my will.

After so many years, I thought I'd gotten over it all. I hadn't thought about it in a long time, not in the way I was.

"Precious, let me take you to bed so I can ask everyone to leave. The party is over," John stated.

I wasn't going to argue. There wasn't a chance that I was going to be able to act like I hadn't just relived the worst time of my life.

"Okay, John," I whispered.

He hoisted me up and carried me to the mattress. The look in his eyes told me he was struggling to hold it together as much as I was, but he walked out of the room with his back straight. It felt like he was gone forever, but was more than likely only a few minutes. He climbed up next to me before pulling me tightly against his chest.

We lay there for a long time. Neither of us spoke, just shared comforting, lingering touches.

"I believe you."

They were the first words John had said since he'd told the guests to leave.

"I am going to delay my treatment so I can be here to take care of you," he whispered as his hands wandered over my back and arms.

"No. It's okay. I'll be okay. I've dealt with this for a long time. I can do it a while longer," I said, not wanting to him to put his life on hold for me.

"The only way I'll go is if you see someone while I'm gone. I'll get help for my problems if you get help for your past." John leaned up on an elbow so he could look down at me.

"I can do that. When we meet again we will both be in a better place," I said, cupping his cheek.

He slowly lowered his head until his lips pressed to mine in a gentle kiss.

We spent the rest of the night touching and kissing. At one point we made love, slow and tender in the dark.

When the sun rose, John got up and packed a few items into a bag to take with him to the treatment center.

"I'll miss you every second I am gone," John said while holding me in his arms.

"Me too," I whispered, but stepped back.

It was going to be hard being apart, but we could do it.

John grabbed my hands in his and sighed. Slowly, he stepped back, then again until our arms were stretched between us. Finally, our fingers slipped apart. He frowned and spun around to walk briskly to the door, closing it softly behind him.

I was glad he'd left the way he had; it made it easier and stopped me from keeping him from going.

Jennifer showed up shortly after he'd left.

"Oh, babe, you look terrible," she said when I opened the door to let her in. "He left already?"

"Yeah. It's for the best." I nodded and moved into the living room.

It was a hot mess. There were half-filled glasses everywhere, along with plates covered with food. The kitchen wasn't any better either. I had a lot of work to do, but it would help keep my mind off everything so I was grateful.

"Well, let's get to cleaning up then," Jennifer said, going into the kitchen, presumably to retrieve bags. When she returned, she handed one to me.

I looked at her and she smiled before getting started. While I expected her to ask what had happened the night before, I was happy that she hadn't brought it up.

By the time everything was back to normal, I plopped onto the couch exhausted and Jennifer followed suit, leaning her head against the back.

"What do you say we go get a drink and some food?" she asked, rolling her head to the side to look at me.

"Sounds good. I'm starving. I also need a shower desperately. What if I meet up with you once I rinse off the stink?" I said, trying to find the energy to get up. It would be good to go out for a little while though.

"Fine. I should probably do the same and it'd be a perfect time for an early dinner," she said, looking at her wrist watch.

I looked at the clock on the wall and was surprised to see how much time had passed while we cleaned.

"All right. Up we go," I said, slapping a hand on Jennifer's thigh.

"Okay. Pull me up," she demanded holding out both her hands.

I laughed and tugged her off the couch.

She left and I jumped in the shower. The warm water felt heavenly as it washed away food, drinks and sweat that had accumulated.

When I got out, I felt much more energetic. After pulling my hair into a ponytail, I dressed in jeans and a silk top with a pair of low heels. Grabbing my purse and phone, I left to meet Jennifer.

She was already at the restaurant when I arrived. The table she'd claimed was in a quieter part so we could still talk without having to shout.

Once we ordered, she took a drink of her soda and gave me a serious look.

"So, do you want to talk about what happened last night?" she asked, putting the glass back down.

"Not really. Let's just say I saw a ghost from the past and didn't want to entertain people anymore. One day I'll tell you all about it, but it's still raw right now," I admitted.

"Oh hell, I understand that. When you're ready to talk, I'll be here. Now how about we talk about all those presents you got?" She quickly changed the subject and I was grateful.

The rest of our meal passed as we chatted about the wedding, or lack of one, and the pros and cons in her eyes. By the time we were done, I was still against having one. Look at how well the engagement party had gone, after all.

"Let's meet up for something fun tomorrow," Jennifer suggested as we walked out of the restaurant.

"I don't know. I might just stay home and veg. I'll call the shelter and see if they need some help, too, since John is gone," I said. I didn't know if I would have the energy to keep up with her again so soon.

"Oh, you are so boring," she teased. "Well, if you get tired of being alone and want some company, you know my number. Don't stay in that house the whole time John is gone."

"I won't. I promise." I knew I had to find a counselor to talk to and that'd give me a reason to get out as well. Plus, the shelter would keep me plenty busy, or I hoped they would since it was all I had besides pestering Jennifer to keep me company.

"Later!" She waved and wandered off to her car.

I headed home with thoughts of lounging on the couch and catching up on some television shows. After parking in the garage, I walked up to the house and unlocked the front door, then walked inside. I put my purse down and flipped on the light.

"What the..." I yelped, jumping back.

Mariah leaned against the back of the couch in a tight pair of black pants and a matching low-cut top with a glass of wine in her hand. She wore heels that had to be at least four inches tall with bright red soles peeking out.

"About time you got home," she said, crossing her ankles where they were stretched out in front of her.

"Why are you here? How'd you get in?" I asked nervously.

"Oh, where to start..." She trailed off before taking a large swallow of wine. "How about you come in and get comfortable. We are going to be here a while."

"Uh... That's okay. I'm good here," I said, not wanting to get any closer to her.

"I insist." She pushed off the couch, and it was only then that I saw in her other hand she had a large knife. "Don't be stupid. Go sit down."

Swallowing hard, I stepped widely around her and sat down on the edge of a cushion. She sat across from me on the coffee table, wine glass still in one hand, knife in the other.

"Since John couldn't see that you were bad for him, I decided to help him see what a bad decision he was making. He needs a strong woman. An employed woman who can not only take care of herself, but provide for the household," she started, as if we were in the middle of a conversation already.

I tried to bite my tongue and not interrupt, but I couldn't.

"He needs a woman who loves him," I said, repeating the words he'd told me numerous times. "The rest will work itself out."

"*I* love him. I could take care of him better than you would ever be able to. I thought he'd leave you once you lost your pathetic job, but he didn't, did he?" Mariah clenched her jaw as she tapped the knife length along her thigh. Her knuckles were white from holding it so tightly.

When I refused to answer, she let out a suffering sigh and took another swig from her glass.

"He didn't even care that holy people were trying to tell you how disgusting you are."

"You know as well as I do that John is also part of the lifestyle." I shook my head, not understanding why she thought any of this would work.

"No!" she shouted suddenly making me slide back on the couch. "No, John doesn't need that in his life. He just thinks he needs to live that way. When we were together he learned that sex could be just as good without it. Our relationship was just as wonderful without it. I never planned to be submissive to him for long."

I pressed my lips together in order not to speak. Obviously, she wasn't going to listen to anything I had to say about BDSM and it seemed to upset her. That was the last thing I wanted to do.

"That fool even let you become friends with his ex-girlfriend simply because it made you happy. I would never have allowed that to happen if... *when* he is mine." She shook her head at her slip and swallowed more alcohol as if that was what she needed. The glass was already more than half empty, so I didn't think it was going to help her, but she didn't ask my opinion.

"I was trying to be the better person," I admitted.

She had truly fooled me. This wasn't the woman I'd hung out with, not at all.

"Becoming your friend allowed me to get close enough to get a copy of your house key without you even knowing. It was your stupidity that let me slip in every night and watch you as you slept," she said with a sick smirk. "Do you know how many times I thought about slitting your throat while you were asleep?"

My eyes widened and I swallowed a lump in my throat. Before I could respond, she continued.

"But that would've been too easy, and really quite painful and messy for John to deal with. So I didn't. Instead I planted some photos on his computer. That was when I realized the true depravity of John's connection to you. The two of you are sick, but that's okay. I can make John better. You, however, I can't. After everything, you still hung on. Even thinking your boyfriend was stalking you and taking naked pictures of you for his own disgusting pleasure, you stayed around. I really thought that would be the end. What kind of woman wants to stay with a man like that?" She shook her head and grimaced. "You, apparently. Then somehow you manage to make the most perfect man in the world check himself into some dumb-fuck facility to get help he doesn't need."

She stood and started pacing as her agitation grew to new levels, scaring me even more.

"You! This meek disaster of a woman turned a strong, dominant man into nothing more than a rehab junkie. Do you have any idea how much that upset me? I couldn't say anything, no. I had one last, lovely surprise for you." She laughed menacingly. "It sort of happened by accident. All the time I spent watching you. The hours and hours I tracked you. And I found that I kept running into the same person over and over. We got to talking and it turned out we had some interesting things in common. Hatred for you. Unfulfilled love for someone."

"What are you talking about?" I asked quietly, hesitantly.

"Bryce, you fool. Your own brother had this twisted desire to hurt you and love you at the same time. God, the things he'd do to me when we role-played. I'd play the sad little sister who liked to act like she didn't want it and he'd play the protective brother who'd give her exactly what she wanted but wouldn't admit to."

My stomach flipped and turned and knotted at her words. I didn't want to hear about Bryce and his disgusting wants or desires.

"Oh, you should have seen your face when he walked in the door of your own house. It was priceless. Too bad I didn't have my camera out for that one. It'd be a photo worth hanging on the wall so I could see it every day." She paused to run a hand through her hair and take another swig. "Anyway, he helped me with my little plan you see. He was the one who spread the rumors about you. It took much longer than we anticipated for the word to spread, but after six months it was finally working. More and more of your clients left you a weeping, pathetic mess. Do you have any idea how many clients *John* lost during that time? How much money he lost while he was making sure *you* were okay?"

"I... I didn't know," I admitted. I was so selfish, and it made me feel embarrassed all over again about the whole situation, but I refused to tell her any more.

"Of course you didn't. You don't really care about John. It's all about you," she said, sitting in front of me once more. "I about lost it when that ring showed up on your finger. If it wasn't for Bryce I really would've ended this all much sooner, but he was right to wait and make you suffer."

"What… what are you going to do?" I stuttered as I asked what I really wanted to know.

John was gone. Jennifer wouldn't be coming by since we'd spent all day together. I was at her mercy with no help in sight.

"Why, kill you of course. I tried everything I could to get you to leave and that didn't work. I tried everything I could to get John to see all the reasons why he should leave you — once again, that didn't work. So now I'll just take you out of the picture myself. By the time John gets back he won't even remember who you are," she said, leaning forward quickly enough to grab my shirt and pull my face to hers. Her knife was pressed against my neck. "He didn't actually see Bryce, doesn't know who he is. Just so happens that Bryce is spending some time checked into a wonderful little facility getting to know John and making sure he gets some new ideas about this woman he is supposed to be marrying. Oh, and John will be getting some letters from you saying that you simply can't wait for him and need to move on with your life. Don't worry, doll face, it's all been planned out."

"Mariah, you can't do this," I said shakily.

The glint in her eyes told me she had lost touch with reality. That scared me almost as much as her words.

"I can. I will. In fact…" Mariah was cut off by the front door slamming open.

I hadn't locked it when I'd walked in so it could've been anyone, but I was still surprised to find John standing in the doorway. He looked as handsome as ever in the same clothes he'd left in just that morning. His face was hard and I got an idea of what he looked like in dom mode when I wasn't distracted by what he was doing to me.

"Mariah," John said, glaring at her.

"John? What are you doing here?" Mariah gasped as she yanked me off the couch and spun me around, using me as a shield between them.

"Let go of Alix," he demanded stepping into the room and leaving the front door wide open.

"No. You're angry and you won't touch me with her between us." Mariah yanked me against her chest and moved us a step away from him.

"I won't hurt you. I just want to talk, and it's hard to do that when you are walking away from me with a knife to Alix's throat." John stepped closer.

I gulped when the knife point dug into my neck enough to break the skin. I hadn't even realized it was there until he'd pointed it out. Surprise at seeing him had distracted me.

"No!" Mariah yelled and forced me back farther away from John.

"Look, I'll sit on the couch. I'm not a threat." He moved to sit on the cushion closest to the door. He relaxed back, looking as if it were any other day and nothing unusual was going on. "No, let Alix go so you and I can talk. I can't even see you with her in the way now."

Mariah was breathing hard against me, but after a drawn-out moment, she shoved me to my knees.

"There, you can see me," she said, still holding the knife against my throat.

I could feel a trickle of blood down my neck, but I didn't move. Not wanting to distract John, I kept my eyes on the floor.

"Babe, come sit down. This is ridiculous," John sighed. "Let me rub your shoulders and help you relax like I used to."

I clenched my jaw at those words. He didn't give *me* shoulder massages, but it didn't matter what he said, as long as she moved the knife.

"That does sound good," Mariah admitted with a wistful moan.

"Let Alix go and give me a chance to make you feel good. I've missed you. I know now I need you back in my life." John held out his arms with a pleading look on his face.

"You're not lying to me, are you?" Mariah's voice was begging him to be telling him the truth. Her hand started to shake.

"No, babe, I need you," John said.

Mariah let out a cry and shoved me onto my face as she ran to him. She jumped into his arms.

John sighed loudly as he wrapped his arms around her tightly. In a moment, he had her flipped onto the couch on her stomach. Out of nowhere he pulled a pair of handcuffs and snapped them on her wrists before she could even comprehend what he was doing.

"What the fuck?" Mariah asked, confused.

"Crazy bitch," John muttered as sirens filled the air.

Soon cops were flooding into the room and Mariah had been taken away. Only then did John come to me.

He helped me to my feet, then crushed me to his heaving chest.

People were asking questions and talking loudly, but nothing mattered at all except that I was safely back in his arms.

"I was so scared," he confessed.

"Me too," I whispered back.

He hiked me up and I wrapped my legs around his hips and my arms around his neck.

I didn't even realize I was weeping until he sat down on the couch and murmured soothing words into my hair.

When a cop demanded someone start talking, it was then I spotted Gabe. He shared our story with the officer.

It was strange, sitting and listening to someone recount all that had happened with Mariah. I was surprised to learn that it was Gabe who had found out that it was Mariah who had uploaded the images to John's computer and somehow found a way to track her. They had left a cell phone on a ledge where it wouldn't be noticed while I'd been out and before Mariah had arrived, so they'd heard everything she'd said and had it recorded too.

The policeman said we had plenty of grounds to file numerous charges against her as well as my brother to keep both of them locked up for a long time.

Finally, I could relax in John's arms. Tension eased from him at the words.

It was over.

__Epilogue__

~John~

It was a beautiful day to get married. Bright and sunny, with the woman I loved by my side. We walked hand in hand into the courtroom with Gabe and Jennifer behind us. The procedure was quick and we were officially married. Didn't even take twenty minutes to tie the woman I loved more than life itself to me.

Not even two weeks had passed since the Mariah incident. We had yet to deal with all the legal mess that was going to come with that, but it didn't matter.

We were happy. We had each other and everything was the way it was meant to be.

I would still be going to treatment for my issues, Alix still was meeting with a therapist to help her with her past, but together we would persevere through it. We'd made it this far, we could make it through anything.

Gabe and Jennifer seemed to be getting along quite well, which was interesting. However, that wasn't what I had on my mind when we left the courthouse. After a quick goodbye, I swept Alix into the car and sped home.

"Precious, welcome home," I said, helping her out of the car.

"Glad to be home, Mr. O'Roarke." She smiled brightly at me.

"Only place I want to be right now, Mrs. O'Roarke."

I scooped her up when we got to the door and carried her over the threshold.

We'd completely redone the living room so it didn't even resemble the room that Mariah had soiled with her presence, but I turned and headed to our bedroom.

Setting Alix on the edge of the mattress, I got down on my knees in front of her.

"I have a present for you," I told her and dug in my pocket for it.

"John, I don't want a present. I have everything I want already," she said with a shake of her head, but grinned anyway.

I pulled out the stainless steel ring and held it up to her.

"Your wedding ring, Precious," I said and watched as confusion ran over her features.

It wasn't nearly as beautiful as the pearl ring paired with the band of diamonds she already had.

"I already have one." She scrunched her cute little brows together.

"Ah, but this is a ring for the bedroom." I flipped the ring open to reveal that it was actually two rings hinged together, then slid each ring over her middle fingers, effectively securing her hands together.

"Oh, I see," she breathed, clearly pleased.

"Now stand up, my wife," I demanded.

She got to her feet.

I slowly pulled down the zipper on the back of the floor-length cream-colored strapless dress she'd worn for the wedding. It fluttered to the floor to pool around her feet, revealing the white strapless bra, garter belt and panties underneath.

"Fucking sexy," I rasped, letting a hand drift between her breasts, down her abdomen to slip between her thighs. Drenched. Just as I'd expected; even through the flimsy material I could tell. "Bend over the bed."

She turned around and rested her forearms on the mattress.

"Hmm, beautiful," I sighed, running a hand down her spine. Stepping back, I quickly removed all of my clothing. Quietly, I opened the bedside drawer and pulled out a condom and a container of lube. I put them on the bed, then hooked my fingers in the sides of her panties before yanking them down. "Lift your foot."

She did, first one, then the other.

I tossed the material away. Rubbing my hands along her smooth, silky skin, I stood again and pressed my erection against her ass.

"You ready for this?" I asked, nudging her again.

"God, yes," she whimpered.

The arousal in her voice made a bead of precome leak out of my cock. I rolled the condom on, then lubed it up liberally, along with two of my fingers.

My fingers traced up and down her crease.

A moan filled the room. It could've been either of us; it didn't matter when my fingers found her tight rosebud and slowly pushed inside.

Alix stiffened for a moment, then pushed her hips back against me.

"More," she gasped.

Resting a palm on her lower back, I thrust the fingers in and out of her, opening her up for me. With her clenching down on and around me, it drove me crazy.

While I filled her with my fingers, I stroked myself. My control was already gone. Something about saying vows and binding our lives together had turned me on like crazy.

My fingers slid out and I rubbed around her hole with the head of my cock before thrusting roughly in. I tried to be tender, but couldn't. I needed her badly.

I grabbed hold of her shoulder and pulled her back into each thrust.

She moaned each time I filled her. Her ragged breathing and shaking body told me she was as close as I was. Her hands clawed at the bedding, trying to balance against the hard fuck she was getting even as she forced her body against mine.

"Come," I barked. "Come. Come now!"

She shrieked out her pleasure and tightened even more around me.

I tumbled after her, melding our bodies together; come pulsed out of me and I roared in triumph at claiming my woman. My wife. My life.

~The End~

<u>More Books By Rachael Orman</u>

<u>Rossi Family (Mob Series)</u>
Matteo

<u>In The Moment Series (M/M/F Menage)</u>
Part One – *FREE*
Part Two
Part Three
Part Four
Part Five

<u>Her Series (Biker)</u>
Her Ride (Ryan & Ellis)
Her Journey (Melia & Patrick)
Her Run (Blaze & Monk)

<u>Cravings Series (BDSM)</u>
Lost Desires (Prequel) - *FREE*
Addict - *FREE*
Fiend

<u>Yearning Series (M/F/F Menage)</u>
Yearning Devotion
Yearning Absolution

<u>Other Works</u>
In Flight (M/F/M Menage – Short Story)
Loneliness Ebbs Deep – CoWritten by Adrian J. Smith – F/F
– Monster Erotica
Love is a Mess Anthology – Bar Tryst (F/F Short)

Made in United States
Troutdale, OR
09/13/2023